Alex Koch

Academy architecture and annual architectural review 1894

Alex Koch

Academy architecture and annual architectural review 1894

ISBN/EAN: 9783741190964

Manufactured in Europe, USA, Canada, Australia, Japa

Cover: Foto ©Andreas Hilbeck / pixelio.de

Manufactured and distributed by brebook publishing software
(www.brebook.com)

Alex Koch

Academy architecture and annual architectural review 1894

ACADEMY ARCHITECTURE

AND

Annual Architectural Review,

1894.

EDITED BY

ALEX. KOCH, Architect.

Membre Honoraire de la Société des Peintres et Sculpteurs Suisse, Expert et Membre du Jury à l'Exposition Nationale Suisse, &c.

CONTAINING

I.—A Selection of the most prominent Architectural Drawings hung at the Exhibitions of the **Royal Academy**, London, the **Royal Scottish Academy**, Edinburgh, and the **Glasgow Institute of the Fine Arts**,

PUBLISHED AT "ACADEMY ARCHITECTURE,"

58 THEOBALDS ROAD, LONDON, W.C.

LONDON—SIMPKIN, MARSHALL, HAMILTON, KENT, AND CO., LIMITED.
LEIPZIG—L. FERNAU.
ZURICH—CAESAR SCHMIDT.
PARIS—Librairies—Imprimeries Réunies, 2 Rue Mignon.
BRUSSELS—E. LYON-CLAESEN, 8 Rue Berckmans.
ROME—MODES & MENDEL, 146 Corso.

MADRID—LIBRERIA NACIONAL Y EXTRANJERA, 59 Jacometrezo.
STOCKHOLM—GUSTAF CHELIUS, Hamngatan, 38.
CHRISTIANIA—CAMMERMEYERS BOGHANDEL, Carl Johansgade, 41 & 43.
ST. PETERSBURG—F. V. SZCZEPANSKI, Nevsky Pr. 31.
ATHENS—CARL BECK.
CONSTANTINOPLE—OTTO KEIL, 457 Grand' rue de Pera.

MELBOURNE, SYDNEY & ADELAIDE—GEORGE ROBERTSON & Co.
NEW YORK—CHARLES SCRIBNER'S SONS, 745 Broadway.

ACADEMY ARCHITECTURE

Will be published annually in May.
Parait toutes les années le mois de Mai.
Erscheint jedes Jahr im Monat Mai.

1894. — LIST OF CONTENTS — 1894.

MANUFACTURERS' AND TRADES' DIRECTORY.

(Where not otherwise stated, the address is London.)

LONDON ist der adresse beizufügen wo bloss die Buchstaben des Postdistrikts angegeben sind.
LONDRES est à ajouter à l'adresse dans tous les cas où seulement les lettres du district postal sont données.

* Advertiser in this Volume.

ART METAL WORK :—
*Bostwick Gate and Shutter Co., Ltd., Baldwin's Gardens, Gray's Inn Road, E.C.
Brawn, Thos. & Co., 64 Clement Street, Birmingham.
Evered & Co., Ltd., Drury Lane, London ; and Surrey Works, Smethwick.
Hamilton, A. G., Westminster Works, Doris Street, Kennington Road, S.E.
Jones, John, Walker's Croft, Victoria Station, Manchester.
Longden & Co., 447 Oxford Street, W., and Phœnix Foundry, Sheffield.

ASH CLOSETS :—
Parker, W. F., Worcester Place Works, Oxford.

BLINDS (WINDOW, &c.) :—
Haskins, Snml. & Bros., 22 and 24 Old Street, E.C.
Hodkinson & Co., Ltd., Small Heath, Birmingham.

BRICKS :—
Bracknell Pottery, Brick, and Tile Co., Wick Hill, Bracknell.
Cliff, Joseph & Sons' Branch of the Leeds Fire Clay Co., Ltd., Baltic Wharf, Waterloo Bridge, S.E. ; and 2 and 4 Wharfs, G.N. Goods Station, King's Cross, N.
Dunton Green Brick & Tile Works, Limited, Dunton Green, near Sevenoaks.
Eastwood & Co., Ltd., Belvedere Road, Lambeth, S.E.
Ellis, Partridge & Co., Grey Friars, Leicester ; and 200 Phœnix Street, St. Pancras, N.W. ; and at Bristol.
Hall, John & Co., Fire-clay Works, Stourbridge.
Hamblet, J., West Bromwich, Staffordshire.
Hartshill Brick and Tile Co., Stoke-upon-Trent.
Skey, G. & Co., Ltd., Wilnecote Works, near Tamworth.
Stanley Bros., Nuneaton.
Trotter, Haines & Corbett, Stourbridge.

BRICK ORNAMENT :—
*Brown, James, Essex Wharf, Durward Street, Whitechapel, E.
Ellis, Partridge & Co., Grey Friars, Leicester ; and 200 Phœnix Street, St. Pancras, N.W. ; and at Bristol.

BUILDERS' IRONMONGERY.
Young & Co., Victoria Works, Wolverhampton ; and Gray's Inn Chambers, 20 Holborn, W.C.

CARVING, WOOD AND STONE :—
Daymond, John & Son, 7, Edward Street, Vauxhall Bridge Road, S.W.
Farmer & Brindley, 63 Westminster Bridge Road, S.E.
Mellier, Ch. & Co., 48, 49, 50 Margaret Street, Cavendish Square, W.
Millson, J. J., 24 City Road, Manchester.
Turpin's Parquet Floor, Joinery, and Wood Carving Co., Ltd., 22 Queen's Road, Bayswater, W.

CEMENT :—
Brotherton & Co., Commercial Buildings, Leeds.
Cliff, Joseph & Sons' Branch of the Leeds Fire Clay Co., Ltd., Baltic Wharf, Waterloo Bridge, S.E. ; and 2 and 4 Wharves, G. N. Goods Station, King's Cross, N.
Ellis, John & ¦ Sons, 8 Market Street, Leicester.

Francis & Co., Ltd., Bridge Foot, Vauxhall, S.W.
Greaves, Bull, & Lakin, Warwick.
Nelson, C. & Co., Ltd., 16 South Wharf, Paddington, W.
Peters Bros., 2 Victoria Mansions, Westminster, S.W.
Rugby Portland Cement Co., Rugby, Warwickshire.

CHIMNEY COWLS :—
*Boyle, R. & Son, Ltd., 64 Holborn Viaduct, E.C.
Fryer, J. D. & W., Brecon, South Wales.
Sutcliffe, Wright, & Son, Globe Sanitary Works, Halifax.

COOKING APPARATUS :—
Longden & Co., 447 Oxford Street, W., and Phœnix Foundry, Sheffield.
Wright, George & Co., 155 Queen Victoria Street, E.C. ; and Burton Weir Works, Rotherham.
*Yates, Haywood & Co., 95 Upper Thames Street, E.C. ; and Effingham Works, Rotherham.

DAMP PROOF COURSES :—
Briggs, W., Chemical Manufacturer, Dundee.
Jennings, G., Lambeth Palace Road, S.E.
White, W., Abergavenny.

DECORATING, &c. :—
Mellier, Ch. & Co., 48, 49, 50 Margaret Street, Cavendish Square, W.
Pitman & Son, 30 Newgate Street, E.C.

DISINFECTING APPARATUS :—
Manlove, Alliott & Co., Ltd., Bloomsgrove Works, Nottingham.

DOOR SPRINGS AND HINGES :—
*Adams, R., 67 Newington Causeway, S.E.
Newman, William & Sons, Hospital Street, Birmingham.

DRAIN TESTS :—
Pain, J. & Sons, 9 St. Mary Axe, E.C.

EARTH CLOSETS :—
Parker, W. F., Worcester Place Works, Oxford.

ELECTRICITY :—
Brush Electrical Engineering Co., Ltd., Belvedere Road, Lambeth, S.E.
Edison, Swan, Co., Ltd., 14 St. Ann's Square, Manchester.
Henney, Geo. F., 156 Sloane Steeet, S.W.
Laing, Wharton, & Down, 32a New Bond Street, W.
Lawrence, Scott, & Co., Ltd., Gothic Works, Norwich.
Mellier, Ch. & Co., 48, 49, 50, Margaret Street, Cavendish Square, W.
*Middleton, V. G., 3 Princes Mansions, Victoria Street, S.W.
South, Harry, 10 & 12 Garrick Street, Covent Garden, W.C.

ELECTRIC FITTING MANUFACTURERS :—
Brawn, Thos. & Co., 64 Clement Street, Birmingham.
Mellier, Ch. & Co., 48, 49, 50 Margaret Street, Cavendish Square W.

ENGINES (GAS) :—
Robey & Co., Ltd., Globe Works, Lincoln.

FANLIGHT OPENERS :—
*Adams, R., 67, Newington Causeway, S.E.
Hill, J., 100a Queen Victoria Street, E.C.

FIBROUS PLASTER :—
*Jones, Fredk. & Co., Silicate Cotton Works, Perren Street, Kentish Town, N.W.

FIREPROOF FLOORING :—
British Metal Expansion Co., Ltd., Stranton Works, West Hartlepool ; London Agents : Rownson Drew & Co., 113 Queen Victoria Street, E.C.
Dennett & Ingle, 5 Whitehall, S.W.
Fawcett, Mark, & Co., 50 Queen Anne's Gate, Westminster, S.W.
Homan & Rodgers, 17 Gracechurch Street, E.C.
*Jones, Fredk. & Co., Silicate Cotton Works, Perren Street, Kentish Town, N.W.
Lindsay, W. & Co., 23 Queen Anne's Gate Westminster, S.W.
Wilkinson, W. B. & Co., 15 Great George Street, Westminster. S.W.

GAS FITTINGS :—
Brawn, Thos. & Co., 64 Clement Street, Birmingham.

GAS GOVERNORS :—
Shaw, Joseph, Albert Works, Huddersfield.

GATES, RAILINGS (IRON), &c. :—
*Bostwick Gate and Shutter Co., Ltd., Baldwin's Gardens, Gray's Inn Road, E.C.
British Metal Expansion Co., Ltd., Stranton Works, West Hartlepool ; London Agents : Rownson Drew & Co., 113 Queen Victoria Street, E.C.
Wragge, George, 156 Chapel Street, Salford, Manchester.
Wright, George & Co., 155 Queen Victoria Street, E.C. ; and Burton Weir Works, Rotherham.
*Yates, Haywood & Co., 95 Upper Thames Street, E.C., and Effingham Works, Rotherham.

GLASS (STAINED, PAINTED, &c.) :—
Farmiloe, G. & Sons, 34 St. John Street, West Smithfield, E.C.
Gibbs, Alexander, 21 Bloomsbury Street, W.C.
Hemming, A. O., 47 Margaret Street, Cavendish Square, W.
Kelley & Co., 45 Tabernacle Street, Finsbury, E.C.
Lazenby, Geo. & Co., Stained Glass Works, Leeds Bridge, Leeds.
Lee, John R. & Co., Ltd., Swallow Street, Birmingham.
Nicholls & Clarke, 6 High Street, Shoreditch, E.
Shrigley & Hunt, John-o'-Gaunt's Gate, Lancaster.

GLAZING :—
Braby, Fredk. & Co., Ltd., Fitzroy Works, 352 to 364 Euston Road, N.W.
Grover & Co., Ltd., Britannia Works, Wharf Road, City Road, N.
Helliwell & Co., 9 Victoria Street, S.W., and Patent Glazing Works, Brighouse, Yorks.
Mellowes & Co., Corporation Street, Sheffield.
Pennycook Patent Glazing Co., 11 West Regent Street, Glasgow.
Rendle, W. E. & Co., Westminster Chambers, 5 Victoria Street, S.W.
Shelly & Co., 55 Lionel St., Birmingham.

GRANITE :—
Fenning & Co., 3 Salters' Hall Court, Cannon Street, E.C.
Macdonald, Alex. & Co., Ltd., 373 Euston Road, N.W.
West of England Granite Co., Penryn, Cornwall.
Wright, James & Sons, Royal Granite Works, Aberdeen.

HEATING

Boyd, Jas. & Sons, Macdowall Street, Paisley.
Constantine, J. & Son, The Convoluted Stove Works, Stockport Street, Manchester.
Crone &, James & Sons, 55 Abercorn Street, Glasgow
*De la Plez, R. P., Fairfield Street, Fairfield, Liverpool.
*Gibbs, Benton & Co., Ltd., St. James' Works, Mill Street, Liverpool, and Ethel Street, Birmingham.
Haden, G. N. & Sons, Trowbridge, Wilts, and 123 Cromer Street, W.C.
Hartley & Sugden, Ltd., Halifax.
Hope, H., 55 Lionel Street, Birmingham.
Jennings, G., Lambeth Palace Road, S.E.
*Jones & Attwood, Stourbridge.
Longden & Co., Phœnix Foundry, Sheffield.
Messenger & Co., Loughborough.
Newnham, Wood & Dyson, Beeston Road, Leeds.
*Parkes, Charles E. S., 103 Bromsgrove Street, Birmingham.
Saunders, S., 93 and 95, Upper Moss Lane, Hulme, Manchester.
Shorland, E. H. & Brother, Drake Street Works, Stretford Road, Manchester.
Wenham Co., Ltd., Upper Ogle Street, Fitzroy Square, W.
Wright, George & Co., 155 Queen Victoria Street, E.C.; and Burton Weir Works, Rotherham.

HORTICULTURAL BUILDINGS :—

Boyd, Jas. & Sons, Macdowall Street, Paisley.
Hope, H., 55 Lionel Street, Birmingham.
Messenger & Co., Loughborough.
*Parkes, Charles E. S., 103 Bromsgrove Street, Birmingham.
Richardson, W. & Co., North of England Horticultural Works, Darlington.

JOINERY :—

Boyd, James & Sons, Macdowall Street, Paisley.
*Elliott, S., Albert Moulding Mills & Joinery Works, Newbury.
Mellier, Ch. & Co., 48, 49, 50 Margaret Street, Cavendish Square, W.
Sage, F. & Co., 58 to 62 Gray's Inn Road, W.C.
Turpin's Parquet Floor, Joinery & Wood-carving Co., Ltd., 22 Queen's Road, Bayswater, W.

KITCHEN RANGES:—

*Yates, Haywood & Co., 95 Upper Thames Street, E.C., and Effingham Works, Rotherham.

LAUNDRY APPLIANCES :—

Bradford, Thos. & Co., Crescent Iron Works, Salford, Manchester.
Manlove, Alliott & Co., Ltd., Bloomsgrove Works, Nottingham.

LIFTS, ELEVATORS, HOISTS, &c. :—

Attwood, A. & Co., Canal Head Foundry & Engineering Works, Ulverston.
Haskins, Saml. & Bros., 22 and 24 Old Street, E.C.
Mallinson, William, Blake Street, Stretford Road, Manchester.
*Otis Elevator Co., Ltd., 4 Queen Victoria Street, E.C.
Richmond, Joseph & Co., 30, Kirby Street, Hatton Garden, E.C.
Stones, John, "Rosside," Ulverston.
Waygood, R. & Co., Falmouth Road, Great Dover Street, S.E.
Youngs, Ryland Street Works, Birmingham.

LIGHTNING CONDUCTORS :—

Bailey, W. H. & Co., Albion Works, Salford, Manchester.
Blackburn, J., Gresham Works, Nottingham.
Bowker, Wm. & Co., Spring Street, Huddersfield.

LIME, SAND, &c. :—

Cliff, Joseph & Sons' Branch of the Leeds Fire Clay Co., Ltd., Baltic Wharf, Waterloo Bridge, S.E.
Ellis, John & Sons, 8 Market Street, Leicester.
Greaves, Bull, & Lakin, Warwick.
Parry, H. & Co., Kirton Lindsey, Lincolnshire.
Peters Bros., 2 Victoria Mansions, Westminster, S.W.
Rugby Portland Cement Co., Rugby, Warwickshire.

LOCKS AND LATCHES:—

Boobbyer, J. H. & Sons, 13 & 14 Stanhope Street, W.C.
Hill, J. 119a Queen Victoria Street, E.C.
Tann, John. 11 Newgate Street, E.C.
Withers, Samuel & Co., Park Works, West Bromwich.
Young & Co., Victoria Works, Wolverhampton, and Gray's Inn Chambers, 20 Holborn, W.C.

MARBLE :—

De Grelle Houdrett & Co., 130 London Wall, E.C.
Emley & Sons, Ltd., Newcastle-upon-Tyne.
Farmer & Brindley, 63 Westminster Bridge Road, S.E.
Galbraith & Winton, 48 Kelvin Street, Glasgow.
Good, J. & E., Phœnix Steam Marble Works, Millbay Road, Plymouth.
Lomas, R. G., King Street, Derby.

MARBLE CHIMNEY PIECES:—

*Yates, Haywood & Co., 95 Upper Thames Street, E.C., and Effingham Works, Rotherham.

MOSAIC WORK:—

Burke & Co., 17 Newman Street, Oxford Street, Dorset.
Carter & Co., Encaustic Tile Works, Poole, Dorset.
De Grelle Houdrett & Co., 130 London Wall, E.C.
Ebner, Jos. F., 150 Old Street, St. Luke's, E.C.
Salviati & Co., 213 Regent Street, W.
Swift, George, 45 The Temple, Dale Street, Liverpool.
Turpin's Parquet Floor, Joinery, & Wood-carving Co., Ltd., 22 Queen's Road, Bayswater, W.

PARQUET FLOORING :—

Arrowsmith, Arthur J. & Co., 80 New Bond Street, W.
De Grelle Houdrett & Co., 130 London Wall, E.C.
Ebner, Jos. F., 150 Old Street, St. Luke's, E.C.
Mellier, Ch. & Co., 48, 49, 50 Margaret Street, Cavendish Square, W.
Turpin's Parquet Floor, Joinery and Wood-carving Co. Ltd., 22 Queen's Road, Bayswater, W.

PAVEMENT LIGHTS :—

St. Pancras Iron Work Company, St. Pancras Road, N.W.
*Wilson, H. & Co., 117 Charterhouse Street, E.C.

PIPES:—

Cliff, Joseph & Sons' Branch of the Leeds Fire Co., Ltd., Baltic Wharf, Waterloo Bridge, S.E.
Stanley Brothers, Nuneaton.

PLASTERING (ORNAMENTAL, &c.):—

Adamant Co. Ltd., 105 Colmore Row, Birmingham.
Battiscombe and Harris, 49 and 50 Great Marylebone Street, Portland Place, W.
British Metal Expansion Co., Ltd., Staunton Works, West Hartlepool; London Agents: Rownson, Drew & Co., 113 Queen Victoria Street, E.C.
Jackson, G & Sons, 49 Rathbone Place, W.
*Jones, Fredk. & Co., Silicate Cotton Works, Perren Street, Kentish Town, N.W.
Mellier, Ch. & Co., 48, 49, 50 Margaret Street, Cavendish Square, W.
Plastic Decoration Co., 21 Wellington Street, Strand, W.C.

PLATE GLASS :—

De Grelle Houdrett & Co., 130 London Wall, E.C.

ROOFING FELT :—

Engert & Rolfe, Ltd., Felt Works, Barchester Street, Poplar, E.

ROOFS AND BUILDINGS (IRON):—

Braby, Fredk. & Co., Ltd., Fitzroy Works, 352-364, Euston Road, N.W.
Humphreys, Ltd., Iron Buildings Works Knightsbridge, Hyde Park, S.W.
Marshall & Hatch, Bingfield Iron Works, York Road, King's Cross, N.
Motley & Green, St. George's Works, Great George Street, Leeds.
St. Pancras Iron Work Company, St. Pancras Road, N.W.

ROOFS (ZINC, COPPER, AND LEAD):—

Braby, Fredk. & Co., Ltd., Fitzroy Works, 352-364 Euston Road, N.W.
Helliwell & Co., Brighouse, Yorkshire, and 9 Victoria Street, S.W.

SAFES AND STRONG-ROOM DOORS :—

Tann, John, 11 Newgate Street, E.C.
Taunton, J. & J., Belgrave Works, Sherbourne Road, Birmingham.
Whitfield, F. & Co., Oxford Street, Birmingham.
Withers, Samuel & Co., Park Works, West Bromwich.

SANITARY APPLIANCES :—

*Adams, R., 67 Newington Causeway, S.E.
Andrew & Nanson, Brixton Road, S.W.
Bowes, Scott, & Western, Broadway Chambers, Westminster, S.W.
*Boyle, R. & Son, Ltd., 64 Holborn Viaduct, E.C.
Clark, T. & C. & Co., Shakespeare Foundry, Wolverhampton.
Cliff, Joseph & Sons' Branch of the Leeds Fire Clay Co., Ltd., Baltic Wharf, Waterloo Bridge, S.E.
Duckett, J. & Son, Burnley, Lancashire.
Farmiloe, G. & Sons, 34 St. John Street, West Smithfield, E.C.
Hughes & Lancaster, Acrefair, Ruabon, and Albany Buildings, 47 Victoria Street, Westminster, S.W.
Jennings, G., Stangate, Lambeth, S.E.
Jones, Browning & Co., Farnworth, Widnes.
Sbanks & Co., Tubal Works, Barrhead, near Glasgow.
Sharpe, Bros. & Co., Ltd., Swadlincote, Burton-on-Trent.
Stiff, J. & Sons, London Pottery, Lambeth, S.E.
Twyford, Thomas W., Cliffe Vale Pottery, Hanley, Staffordshire.
Woodward & Rowley, Swadlincote, near Burton-on-Trent.
Wright, George & Co., 155 Queen Victoria Street, S.E.; and Burton Weir Works, Rotherham.
*Yates, Haywood, & Co., 95 Upper Thames Street, E.C., and Effingham Works, Rotherham.

SANITARY WARE:—

Burn & Baillie, 14 Newcastle Street, Farringdon Street, E.C.
Cliff, Joseph & Sons' Branch of the Leeds Fire Clay Co., Ltd., Baltic Wharf, Waterloo Bridge, S.E.
Hartshill Brick & Tile Co., Stoke-upon-Trent.
Jennings, G., Stangate, Lambeth, S.E.
Knowles, J. & Co., 36 King's Road, St. Pancras, N.W.
Sbanks & Co., Tubal Works, Barrhead, near Glasgow.
Skey, G. & Co., Ltd., Wilnecote Works, near Tamworth.
Stanley, Bros., Nuneaton.
Stiff, J. & Sons, Lambeth, S.E.
Twyford, Thomas W., Cliffe Vale Pottery Hanley, Staffordshire.
Woodward & Rowley, Swadlincote, near Burton-on-Trent.

SEWAGE AND WATER SYSTEMS:—

Hughes & Lancaster, Albany Buildings, 47 Victoria Street, Westminster, S.W., and Acrefair, Ruabon.

SILICATE COTTON OR SLAG WOOL:—

*Jones, Fredk. & Co, Silicate Cotton Works, Perran Street, Kentish Town, N.W.

SLATES:—

Carter, A. & Co., Liverpool.
Llangollen Slab and Slate Co., Ltd., Llangollen.

SOUNDPROOF FLOORS, &c.:—

*Jones, Fredk. & Co., Silicate Cotton Works, Perran Street, Kentish Town, N.W.

STABLE FITTINGS:—

Musgrave & Co., Ltd., Ann Street Iron Works, and Cromac Foundry, Belfast.
St. Pancras Iron Work Company, St. Pancras Road, N.W.
*Yates, Haywood & Co., 95 Upper Thames Street, E.C., and Effingham Works, Rotherham.
Young & Co., 12 Victoria Street, Westminster, S.W.

STABLE PAVING:—

"Adamantine Clinker," Little Bytham, Grantham.
Cliff, Joseph & Sons' Branch of the Leeds Fire Clay Co., Ltd., Baltic Wharf, Waterloo Bridge, S.E.
St. Pancras Iron Work Company, St. Pancras Road, N.W.
Stanley Brothers, Nuneaton.

STAIRCASES, VERANDAHS, &c.:—

Brawn, Thomas & Co., 64 Clement Street, Birmingham.
Marshall & Hatch, Bingfield Iron Works, York Road, King's Cross, N.
St. Pancras Iron Work Company, St. Pancras Road, N.W.
Wright, George & Co., 155 Queen Victoria Street, E.C.; and Burton Weir Works, Rotherham.

STONE:—

Bath Stone Firms, Ltd., Abbey Yard, Bath.
Ham Hill Stone Co., Norton, Stoke-under-Ham, Somerset.
Lindley Quarries, Mansfield, Notts.
Thompson's Ancaster Quarries Co., Ltd., 11 Elmer Street, Grantham.
Trask, Charles & Sons, Doulting Stone Quarries, Shepton Mallet.

STONE BREAKERS:—

Mason, S. & Co., Leicester.

STOVES, RANGES, MANTELS, &c.:—

Barnard, Bishop, & Barnards, Ltd., Norfolk Iron Works, Norwich: and 95 Queen Victoria street, E.C.
Crosthwaite, R. W., Union Foundry, Stockton-on-Tees.
Jennings, G., Stangate, Lambeth, S.E.
London Warming and Ventilating Co., Ltd., 105 Regent Street, W., "The Quadrant."
Longden & Co., 447 Oxford Street, W., and Phœnix Foundry, Sheffield.
Musgrave & Co., Ltd., Ann Street Iron Works, and Cromac Foundry, Belfast.
Shorland, E. H. & Brother, Drake Street Works, Stretford Road, Manchester.
Teale Fireplace Co. (Teale and Somers), Leeds.
Walker, W. & Sons, Bunhill Row, E.C.
Wright, George & Co., 155 Queen Victoria Street, E.C., and Burton Weir Works, Rotherham.
*Yates, Haywood & Co., 95 Upper Thames Street, E.C., and Effingham Works, Rotherham.

STRUCTURAL IRONWORK:—

Dennett & Ingle, 5 Whitehall, S.W.
Dorman, Long & Co., Ltd., Middlesborough.
Fawcett, Mark & Co., 50 Queen Anne's Gate, Westminster, S.W.
Henderson & Glass, Vulcan Street Iron Warehouses, Liverpool.
Homan & Rodgers, 17 Gracechurch Street, E.C.
Williamson, J. & Co., Midland Foundry, Wellingborough.

TANKS, CISTERNS, &c.:—

Braby, Fredk. & Co., Ltd., Fitzroy Works, 352 to 364 Euston Road, N.W.
Cliff, Joseph & Sons' Branch of the Leeds Fire Clay Co., Ltd., Baltic Wharf, Waterloo Bridge, S.E.
Motley & Green, St. George's Works, Great George Street, Leeds.
Williamson, J. & Co., Midland Foundry, Wellingborough.
Withers, Samuel & Co., Park Works, West Bromwich.

TERRA-COTTA:—

*Clark & Rea, Ltd., Wilderness Works, Wrexham.
Cliff, Joseph & Sons' Branch of the Leeds Fire Clay Co., Ltd., Baltic Wharf, Waterloo Bridge, S.E.
Hamblet, J., West Bromwich, Staffordshire.
Jennings, G., Stangate, Lambeth, S.E.
Pulham & Son, Terra Cotta Works, Broxbourne, and 50 Finsbury Square, E.C.
Skey, G. & Co., Ltd., Wilnecote Works, near Tamworth.
Stanley, Bros., Nuneaton.
Stiff, J. & Sons, London Pottery, Lambeth, S.E.

TILES:—

Bracknell Pottery Brick & Tile Co., Wick Hill, Bracknell, Berks.
Broseley Tile Manufacturers' Association, Broseley, Shropshire.
Caldick, John, Sproutfield Tileries, Stoke-on-Trent.
Carter & Co., Encaustic Tile Works, Poole, Dorset.
Cliff, Joseph & Sons' Branch of the Leeds Fire Clay Co., Ltd., Baltic Wharf, Waterloo Bridge, S.E.
Craven, Dunnill & Co., Ltd., Jackfield, Ironbridge, Shropshire, and 37 Maddox St., Regent St., W.
Dunton Green Brick & Tile Works, Limited, Dunton Green, near Sevenoaks.
Galbraith & Winton, 48 Kelvin Street, Glasgow.
Hamblet, J., West Bromwich, Staffordshire.
Hartshill Brick & Tile Co., Stoke-upon-Trent.
Major, H. J. & C., Ltd., Patent Tile Works, Bridgwater.
Malkin, Edge & Co., Burslem, Staffordshire.
Maw & Co., Ltd., Benthall Works, Jackfield, Salop.
Minton, Hollins & Co., Patent Tile Works, Stoke-upon-Trent.
Prestage & Co., The Milburgh Tileries, Broseley, Salop.
Simpson, W. B. & Sons, 100 St. Martin's Lane, W.C.
Stanley, Bros., Nuneaton.
Warne, C. G., Royal Pottery, Weston-Super-Mare.
Wedgwood, J. & Sons, Etruria, Stoke-on-Trent.

TIMBER:—

Bloore, W., 80–90 Bond Street, Vauxhall, S.W.
Rowland, Bros., Steam Saw Mills, & Fencing Works, Fenny Stratford, Bucks.
Sandell, H. & Sons, Crown Timber Yard, Cornwall Road, Lambeth, S.E.
Stone, Charles, Saw Mills, High Wycombe.
Tealby & Co., Garrison Side, Hull.

TURRET CLOCKS, BELLS, &c.:—

Carr, C., Smethwick.
Joyce, J. B. & Co., Whitchurch.
Potts, W. & Sons, Guildford Street, Leeds.
Smith, John, & Sons, Midland Steam Clock Works, Derby.

VENTILATING:—

*Adams, R., 67 Newington Causeway, S.E.
Baxendale & Co., Miller Street, Manchester.
*Boyle, R. & Son, Ltd., 64 Holborn Viaduct, E.C.
Constantine, J. & Son, The Convoluted Stove Works, Stockton Street, Manchester.
Cormack, James & Sons, 36 Abercorn Street, Glasgow.
*De Ridder, R. P., Fairfield Street, Fairfield, Liverpool.
*Gibbs, Renton & Co., Ltd., St. James' Works, Mill Street, Liverpool, and Ethel Street, Birmingham.
Haden, G. N. & Sons, Trowbridge, Wilts, and 123 Cromer Street, W.C.
Howorth, James & Co., Victoria Works, Farnworth, near Manchester.
Kershaw, A. W. & Co., Custom House Buildings, St. George's Quay, Lancaster.
Kite, C. & Co., Christopher Works, Charlton Street, N.W.
Shorland, E. H. & Brother, Drake Street Works, Stretford Road, Manchester.

WALL AND CEILING COVERINGS:—

Anaglypta Co., 92 and 93 Great Russell Street, W.C., and Queen's Mill, Lancaster.
Cotterell, Bros., 11 Clare Street; 2 and 6 Marsh Street, and 8 Baldwin Street, Bristol.
Doveston, Davey, Hull, & Co., Ltd., Albert Square, Manchester.
*Essex & Co., 116 Victoria Street, Westminster, S.W.
Mellier, Ch. & Co., 48, 49, 50 Margaret Street, Cavendish Square, W.
Pitman & Son, 30 Newgate St., E.C.
Tynecastle Co., Edinburgh, and 14 Rathbone Place, W.
*Walton, F. & Co., Ltd., Lincrusta Manufacturers, 2 Newman Street, W.
*Woollams, W. & Co., 110 High Street, near Manchester Square, W.

WEATHER BARS:—

*Elliott, S., Albert Moulding Mills & Joinery Works, Newbury.

WINDOW FRAMES (IRON):—

*Adams, R., 67 Newington Causeway, S.E.
Hope, H., 55 Lionel Street, Birmingham.
Jones, John, Walker's Croft, Victoria Street, Manchester.
St. Pancras Iron Work Company, St. Pancras Road, N.W.
Wenham & Waters, Ltd., Paragon Works, Croydon.
Wragge, George, 156 Chapel Street, Salford, Manchester.

WINDOWS (REVERSIBLE):—

*Adams, R., 67 Newington Causeway, S.E.

WOOD CHIMNEY-PIECES:—

Battiscombe and Harris, 49 and 50 Great Marylebone Street, Portland Place, W.
Mellier, Ch. & Co., 48, 49, 50 Margaret Street, Cavendish Square, W.
Walker, W. & Sons, Bunhill Row, E.C.
Wright, George & Co., 155 Queen Victoria Street, E.C.; and Burton Weir Works, Rotherham.
*Yates, Haywood & Co., 95 Upper Thames Street, E.C., and Effingham Works, Rotherham.

WOOD FLOORING AND PAVING:—

Charteris & Longley, Earl Street, Westminster, S.W.; Works: Crawley, Sussex.
Ebner, Jos. F., 150 Old Street, St. Luke's, E.C.
Lowe, Roger, L., Britannia Works, Farnworth, Bolton, near Manchester.

Perfection in Improved Patented Specialities of the Building Trades.

VICTOR

53 Highest Awards at Competitive Exhibitions.

Wrought Iron and other Metal Casements and Frames, "Impervious" Patent Warranted Weatherproof.

"Empress Victor" Patent Pneumatic Door Spring and Check.—Strongest at the closed position, best and most reliable, durable and very

neat; can be fixed on either side of door or on right or left hand side; small space only required. Various sizes made.

Panic or Exit Appliances for Instant Egress. The "Exodus" and other Varieties, with or without Outside Handle and Key.

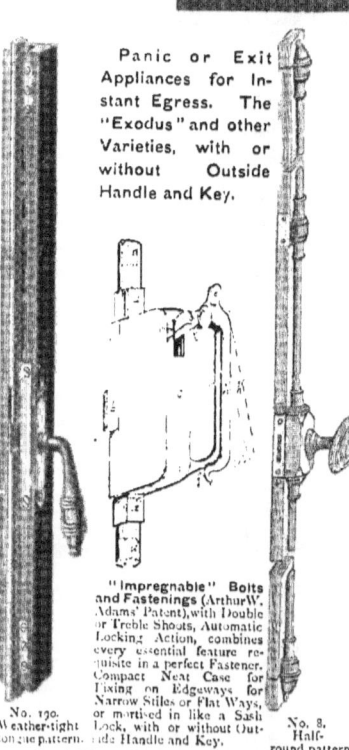

"Impregnable" Bolts and Fastenings (Arthur W. Adams' Patent),with Double or Treble Shoots, Automatic Locking Action, combines every essential feature requisite in a perfect Fastener. Compact Neat Case for Fixing on Edgeways for Narrow Stiles or Flat Ways, or mortised in like a Sash Lock, with or without Outside Handle and Key.

No. 190. Weather-tight tongue pattern.

No. 8, Half-round pattern.

Special Casement Bolts, triple action for casements opening in or out, guaranteed reliable and efficient, new actions.

Write for Lists and Terms for Patent Door Springs, Fanlight and Lantern Light and Skylight Openers, Ventilators (Inlets and Outlets) of every descrip-

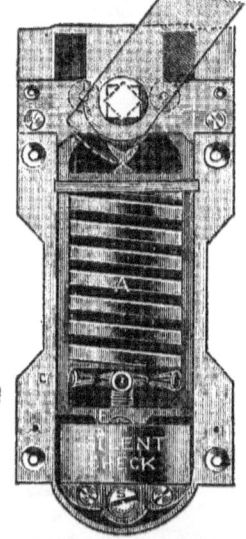

Patent Ventilating Gear for Skylights, Lantern Lights, and other continuous Ranges of Sashes.— Length no object : efficient and reliable in all cases whatever the weight. Modifications to suit all work.

The "Crown"Pattern Floor Hinge for Swing Doors. Made with the Silent Check or without ; also to suit single actions doors closing one way. These celebrated springs belong to the "Victor" Class patents, in which are embodied all recent improvements not to be found in any other kind.

ROBERT ADAMS,

Telegrams—" Robert Adams, London."

Building Trades' Emporium,

67 Newington Causeway, London, S.E.

ROBERT ADAMS' PATENT "UNIVERSAL" FANLIGHT OPENER, with Rod and Handle.

The "Universal" Pattern is an extremely simple, neat, effective, and cheap Fanlight Opener, consisting of a Screw and a universal joint ; the Vertical Rod, which has a tube at the lower end concealing a jointed handle.

The Fanlight is operated by turning the handle (A), first slipping up the cover tube (B). The action is communicated by the rod (A), and nut (F), causing it to traverse the screw (E), thereby acting on the sash by the link (T). The universal joint (D) admits of the rod (A) being angled to any convenient extent for working it (see dotted lines), but when released from the hand the tube drops over and conceals the handle, and the rod hangs vertically

No. 330.

"Another favourite pattern is my Link Motion, No. 114, with Screw at bottom of Rod, passing through the patent enclosed gear regulator. This regulator can also be supplied to revolve the Rod of No. 330.

tion, Gate Hinges and Fittings, Iron Doors, and Gates, Artistic and other Metal Work, Patent "Impervious" Metal Casements and Frames, &c., &c.

ACADEMY ARCHITECTURE
1894.

" Triumph," *Sketch Model for Colossal Group,* ADRIAN JONES, Sculptor.

1643. *Oriel Window, Institute of Chartered Accountants,* JOHN BELCHER, F.R.I.B.A., Architect.

1634. *Northampton Institute, Clerkenwell, Tower and Principal Entrance,* EDWARD W. MOUNTFORD, F.R.I.B.A.,
Architect.

1628. *Bond Street Façade, County Council Offices, Wakefield,* GIBSON AND RUSSELL, Architects.

1626.   *Principal Entrance, County Council Offices, Wakefield*, GIBSON AND RUSSELL, Architects.

1566. *Memorial to the late C. W. Cope, R.A.*, JOHN W. SIMPSON, A.R.I.B.A., Architect.

G

Bird's-eye View from North West of the
New Monastery and Collegiate Buildings
St Lawrences Ampleforth York.

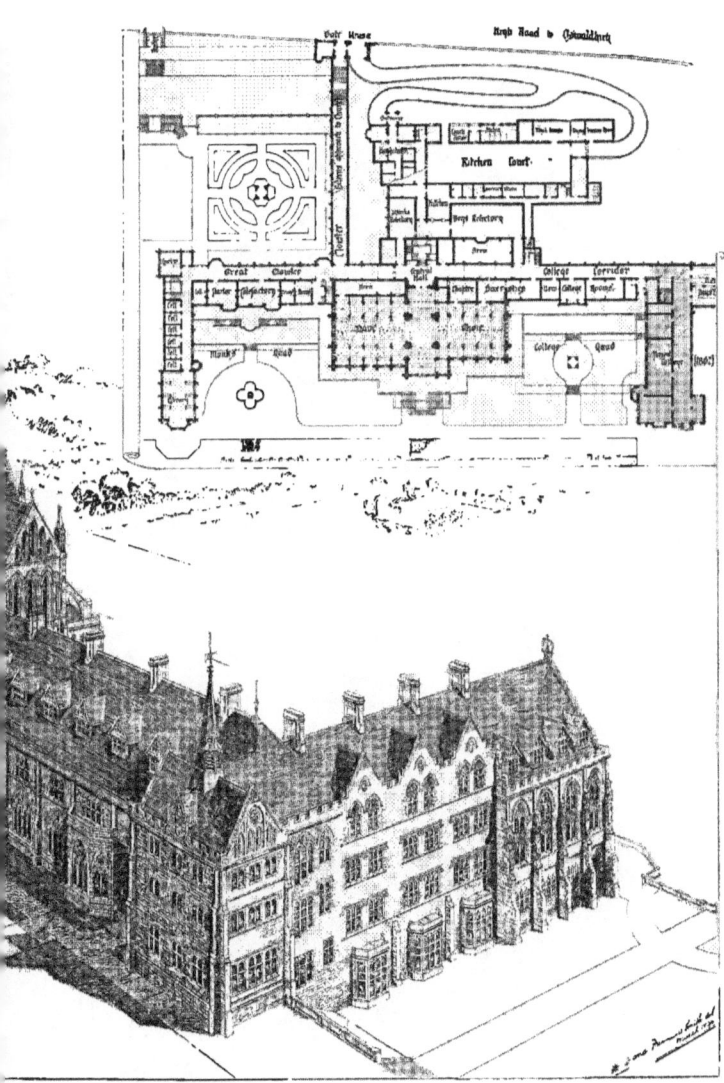

and Collegiate Buildings, St. Lawrence's, Ampleforth,

1644. *Interior of the New Chapel of Radley College*, THOMAS G. JACKSON, A.R.A., Architect.

1575.   *The Victoria Institute, Worcester, Entrance from Foregate Street,* SIMPSON AND ALLEN, Architects.

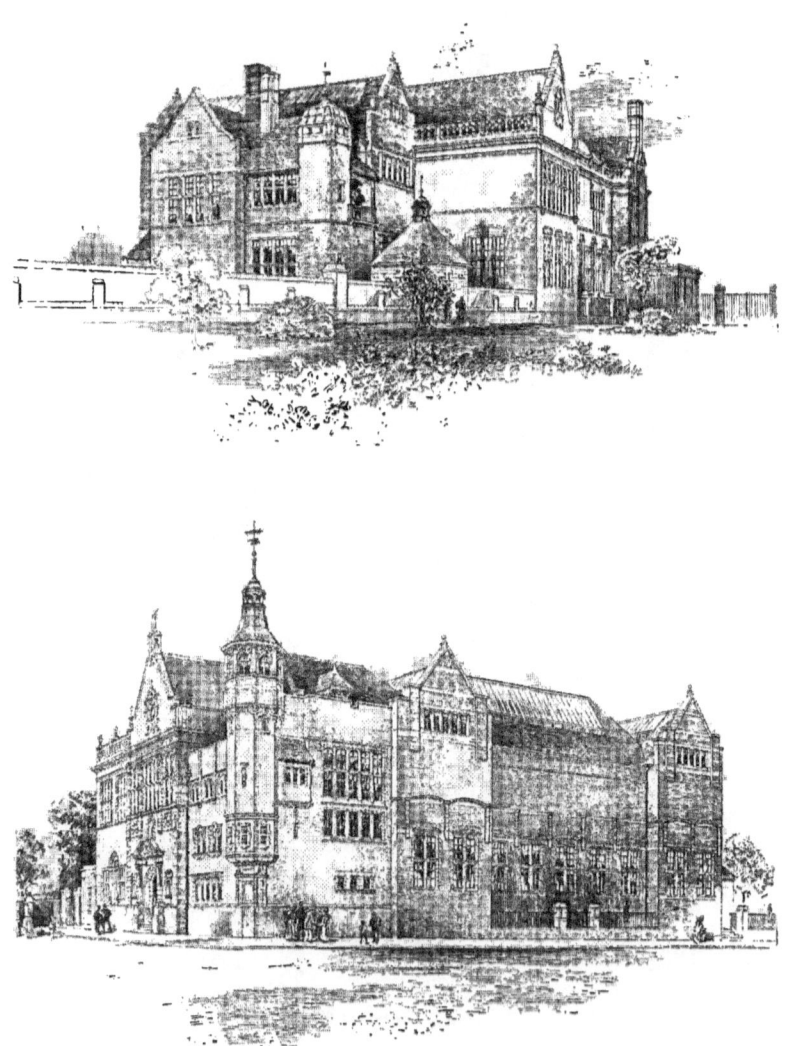

1575. *The Victoria Institute, Worcester, Library Block*, SIMPSON AND ALLEN, Architects.

1575. *The Victoria Institute, Worcester, Schools Block,* SIMPSON AND ALLEN, Architects.

1621. *Restoration of the Chancel, Canewdon Church, Essex,* W. HARGREAVES RAFFLES, Architect.

1567. *A Town House,* CHARLES V. JOHNSON, Architect.

1618. *A small Art School for a Country Town or Suburb,* EDWARD B. LAMB, Architect.

1604. *House recently built at Douglas,* MACKAY H. B. SCOTT, Architect.

House in Wickham Road, Beckenham, ARCHER AND HOOPER, Architects.

1623. *Village Church, Broxburn, West Lothian,* J. GRAHAM FAIRLEY, F.R.I.B.A., Architect.

1557. *Nos.* 126, 127, *and* 128 *Leadenhall Street, E.C., for the P. and O. Steam Navigation Company, Ltd.,*
T. E. COLLCUTT, F.R.I.B.A., Architect.

1709. *Moorgate Court, E.C., for the Ocean Accident and Guarantee Corporation, Ltd.,*
H. HUNTLY-GORDON, A.R.I.B.A., Architect.

1561. *Motcombe, Dorset, for Lord Stalbridge, the Hall,* ERNEST GEORGE AND PETO, Architects.

1561. *Motcombe, Dorset, for Lord Stalbridge, the Morning Room*, ERNEST GEORGE AND PETO, Architects.

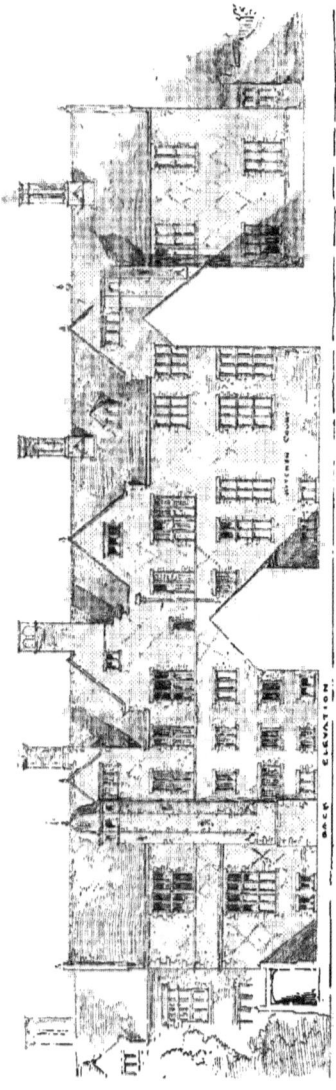

1562. *New Wing to North Mymms, for Walter H. Burns, Esq., Back Elevation,* ERNEST GEORGE AND PETO, Architects.

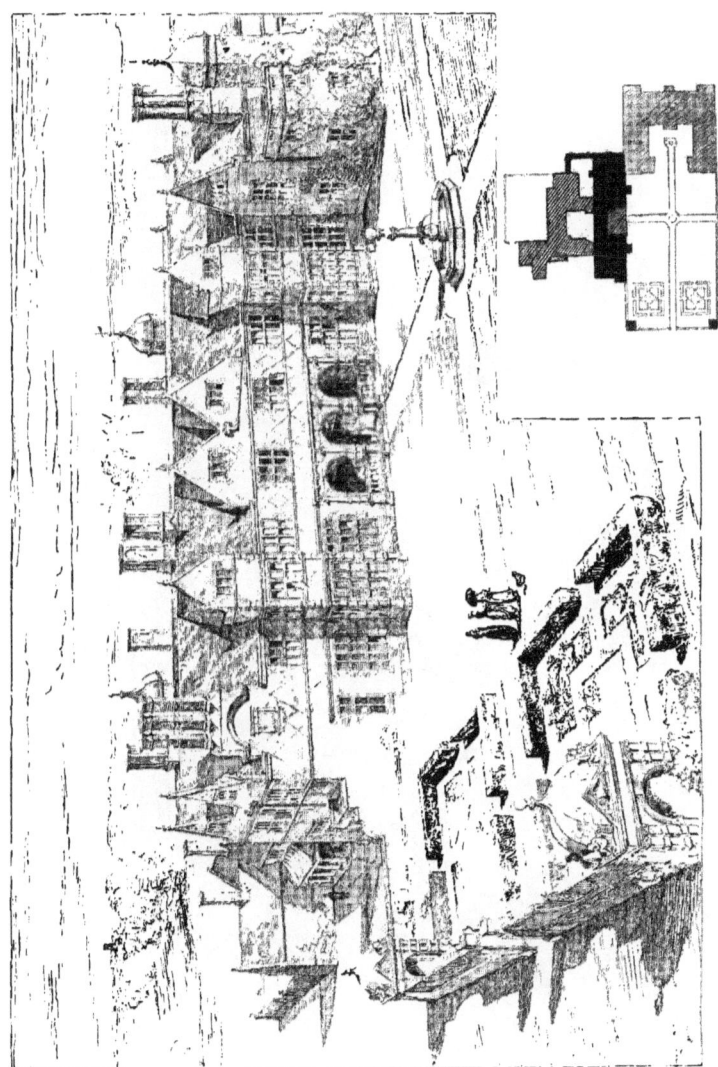

1562. *New Wing to North Mymms, for Walter H. Burns, Esq.,* ERNEST GEORGE and PETO, Architects.

Electric Lighting—V. G. Middleton, 3 Princes Mansions, Victoria Street, S.W

Academy Architecture, 1894.

1549. New Public Offices and Technical Institute, Leyton, Perspective View, FREDERICK H. TULLOCH, A.R.I.B.A., Architect.

1647. *New Premises for the Chester Boat Company, Limited*, THOMAS M. LOCKWOOD and SONS, Architects.

1720. *S'. John's Church, Whittington, Salop, Interior View*, FAIRFAX B. WADE, F.R.I.B.A., Architect

St. John's Church, Whittington, Salop, FAIRFAX B. WADE, F.R.I.B.A., Architect.

1603. *St. John's Church, Bassenthwaite Lake*, DANIEL BRADE, Architect.

1524. *Magdalen College, Oxford, New Choir School*, SIR ARTHUR W. BLOMFIELD, A.R.A., Architect.

1719. *St. John's Church, Whittington, Salop, Exterior View from North-East*, FAIRFAX B. WADE, F.R.I.B.A., Architect.

1691. *Palazzo Notari, Ventimiglia, Italy*, W. D. CARÖE, M.A., Architect.

1532. *Marble Staircase, Glasgow Municipal Buildings*, WILLIAM YOUNG, F.R.I.B.A., Architect.

1699. *Design for Reredos and Altar Rail, Douglas Castle,* H. WILSON, Architect.

1692. *Study for proposed Reredos, Holy Trinity Church, Chelsea,* H. WILSON, Architect.

1693. *Holy Trinity Church, Chelsea, Elevation of Proposed Reredos.* H WILSON, Architect.

1555, 1556. *Church of the Good Shepherd, Gospel Oak,* JAMES BROOKS AND SON, Architects.

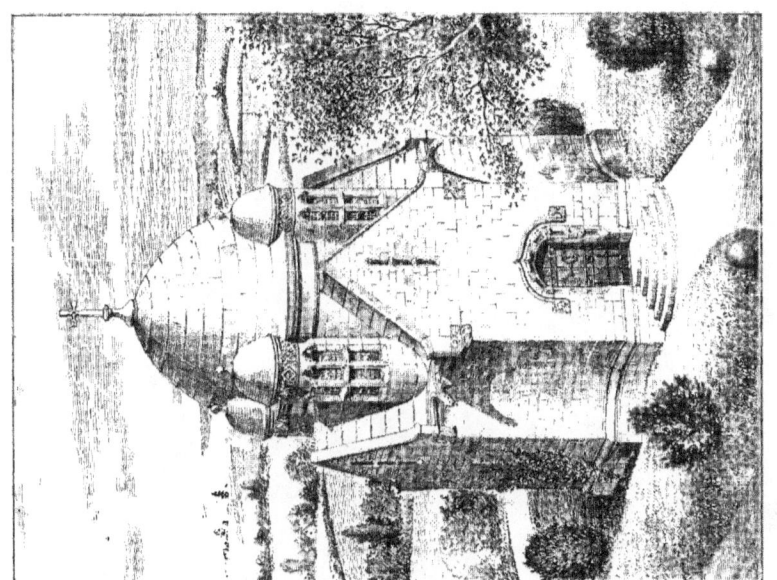

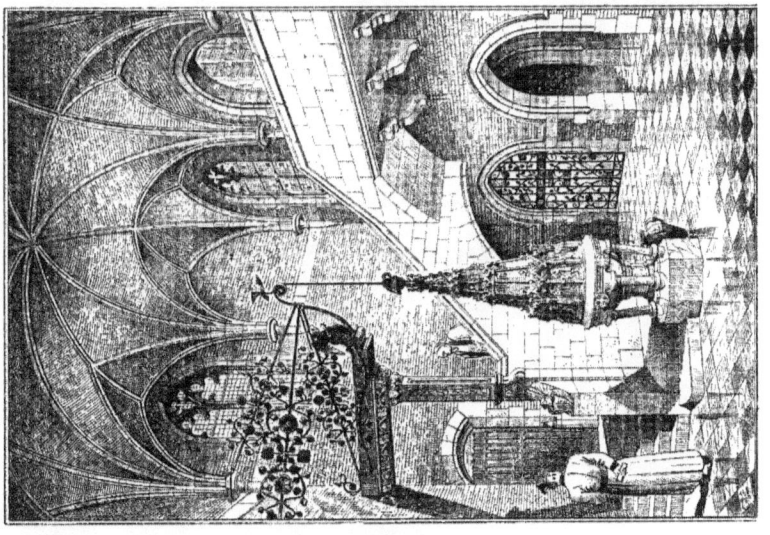

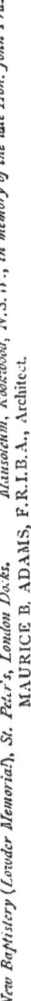

1612. *New Baptistery (Lowder Memorial), St. Peter's, London Docks. Mausoleum, Rookwood, N.S.W., in memory of the late Hon. John Frazer.*
MAURICE B. ADAMS, F.R.I.B.A., Architect.

1539. *New Club House, for Conservative Club, Glasgow,* ROBERT W. EDIS, F.S.A., Architect.

1580. *Newnham College, Cambridge, Pfeiffer Building,* BASIL CHAMPNEYS, B.A., Architect.

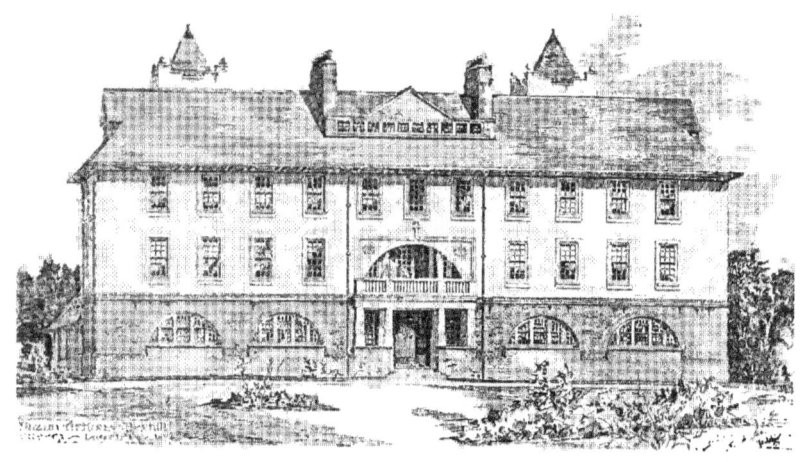

1597. *Nazareth House, Bexhill,* LEONARD STOKES, Architect.

1734. *Design for Entrance Hall and Staircase,* W. TILLOTT BARLOW, A.R.I.B.A., Architect.

1674. *Country School, Armadale, West Lothian*, J. GRAHAM FAIRLEY, F.R.I.B.A., Architect.

1579. *Haslingden Vicarage, Lancashire*, BASIL CHAMPNEYS, B.A., Architect.

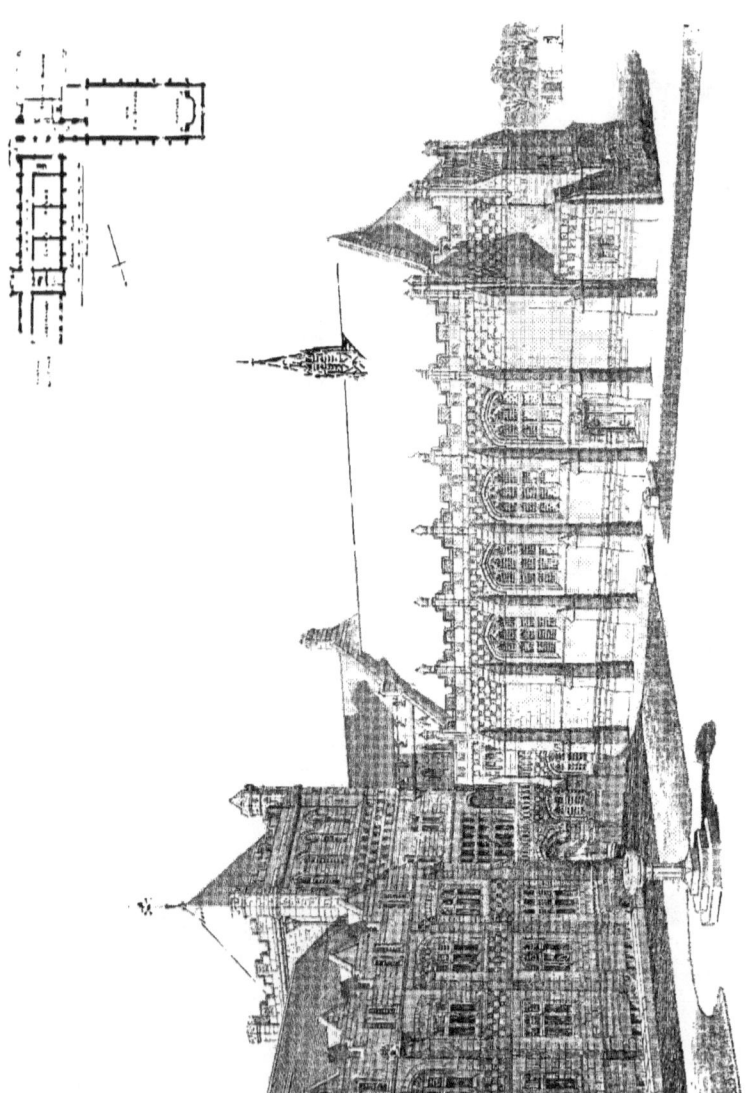

1737.   *A Portion of the New School Buildings, Tonbridge, Kent,* W. CAMPBELL JONES, A.R.I.B.A., Architect.

Slindon Church Staffs.
Basil Champneys B.A.
Architect

1578. *Slindon Church, Eccleshall, Staffs.*, BASIL CHAMPNEYS, B.A., Architect.

1576. *New Houses, Gainsborough Gardens, Hampstead,* HORACE FIELD, Architect.

1717. *House, Disley, Cheshire, for A. Crewdson, Esq.,* JOHN BROOKE, A.R.I.B.A., Architect.

Design for a House, ROBERT A. BRIGGS, F.R.I.B.A., Architect.

1708. *Design for a House,* ROBERT A. BRIGGS, F.R.I.B.A., Architect.

1688. *Proposed Restoration of South Shoebury Church. Freer* CHARLES A. NICHOLSON, M.A., Archiect.

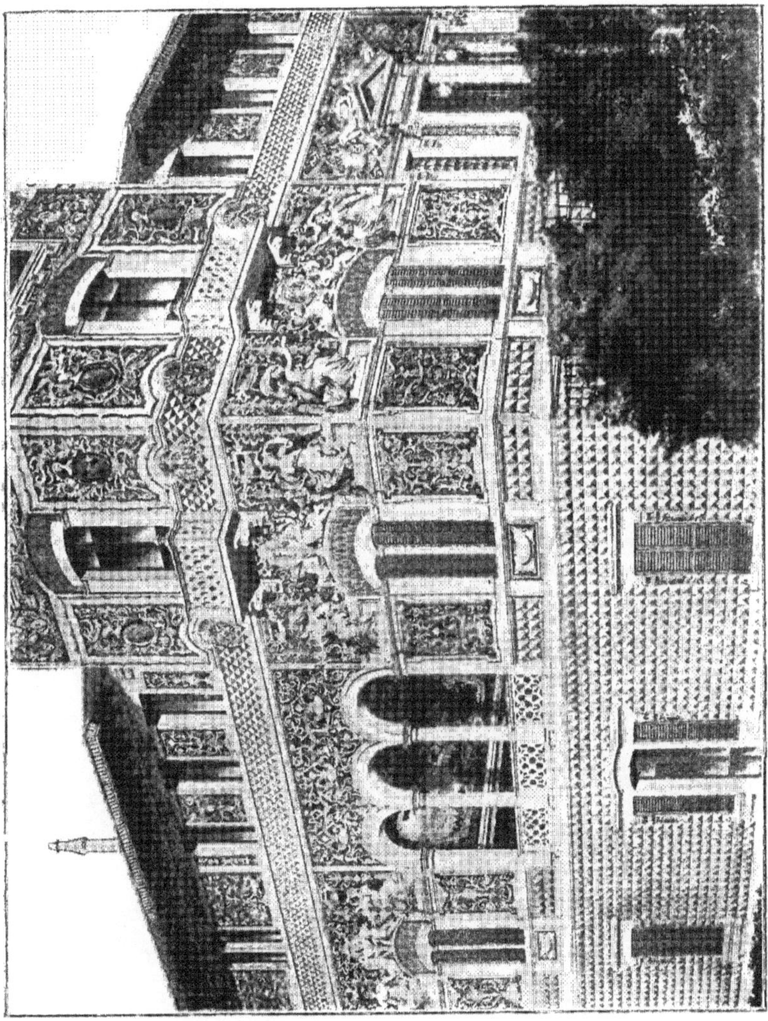

1606. *Design for the Decoration in Graffito of the House of Sn. Guimarães, Lisbon,* BY T. G. CESARE FORMILLI.

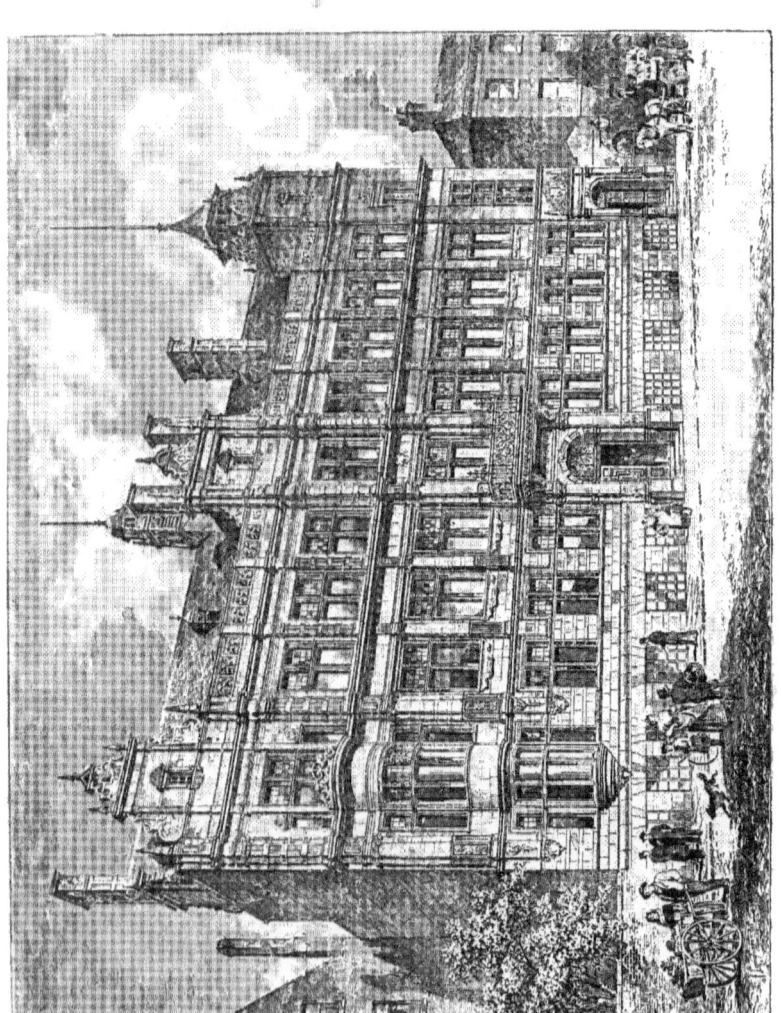

1724. *Salford School Board Offices*, WOODHOUSE AND WILLOUGHBY, Architects.

(For Plans, *see* p. 153.)

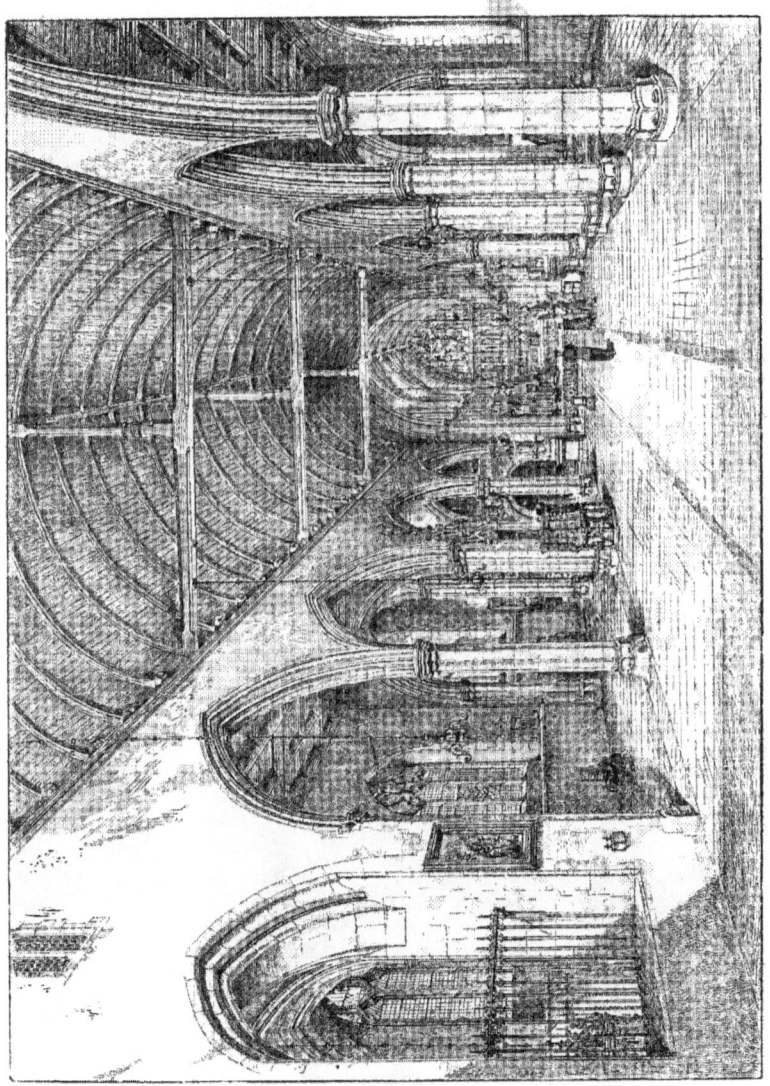

1614. *Wandsworth Church of St. Thomas of Canterbury, Interior,* EDWARD GOLDIE, Architect.

1590. *The Library, H.M. the Queen Regent of Spain's Residence, San Sebastian,*
R. SELDEN WORNUM, F.R.I.B.A., Architect.

1568. *Design for a Frieze*, PATON WILSON, Architect.

1706. *The Gables, Nightingale Lane,* LEONARD J. WILLIAMS, Architect.

1560. · *Bickly Hall Stables, Kent,* ERNEST NEWTON, Architect.

1678. *Design for the Free Library and Technical School, St. Helen's,* GERALD C. HORSLEY, Architect.

1516. *New House, Sharnden, near Mayfield, Sussex, view from South-East*, H. O. CRESSWELL, A.R.I.B.A., Architect.

1517. *New House, Sharnden, near Mayfield, Sussex, view from South-West*, H. O. CRESSWELL, A.R.I.B.A., Architect.
(For Plans, *see* p. 153.)

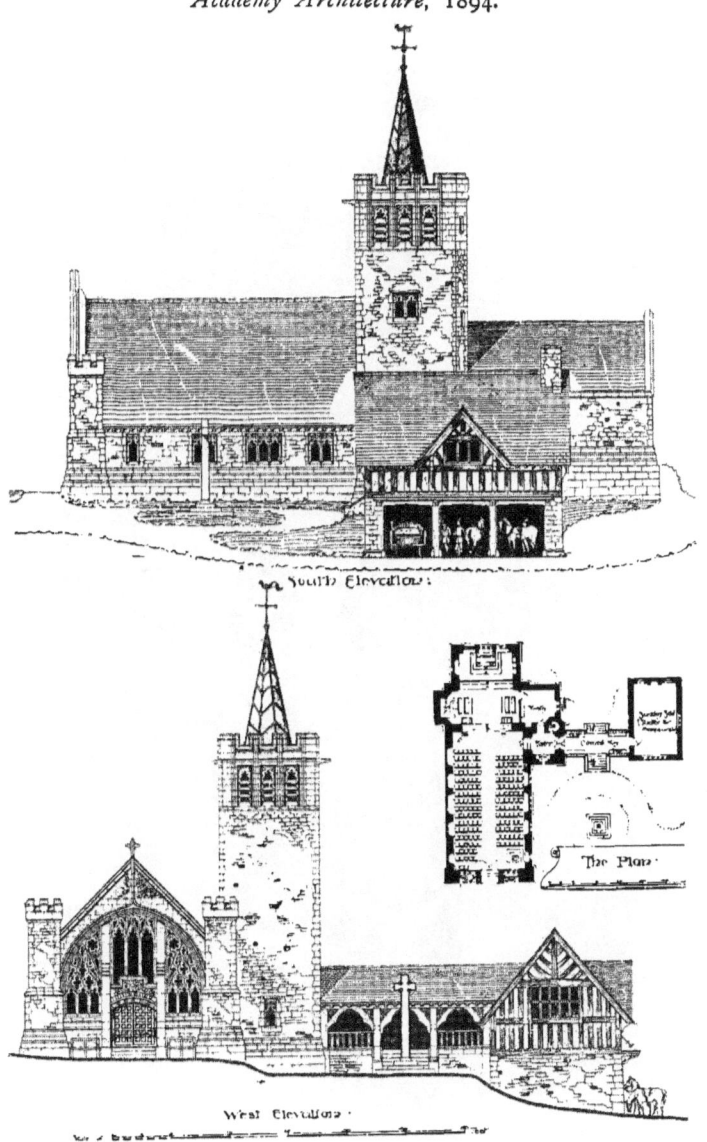

1622. *A Moorland Church, with Sunday School and shelter for carriages*, BANISTER F. FLETCHER, A.R.I.B.A.,
Architect.

1645. *New Lodge and Entrance Gates; Eaton, for His Grace The Duke of Westminster, K.G.,* DOUGLAS AND FORDHAM, Architects.

1633.　*St. Mary's Church, Summerstown, S.W.,* EDWARD W. MOUNTFORD, F.R.I.B.A., Architect.

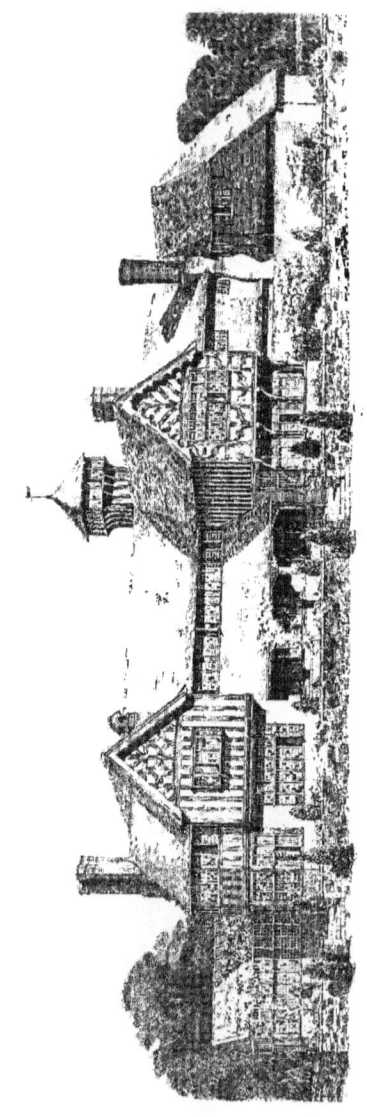

1595. *Garden Front, " Ashcroft," Burnham,* WILLIAM F. UNSWORTH, F.R.I.B.A., Architect.

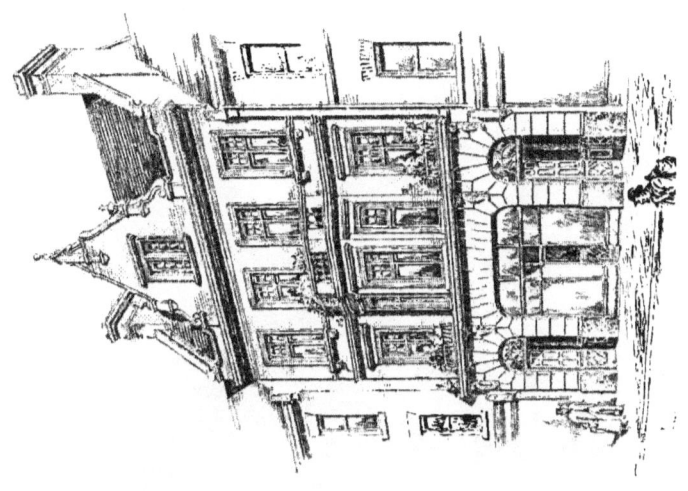

1531. *Proposed Business Premises, Kingsland Road, N.E.,*
CHARLES V. JOHNSON, Architect.

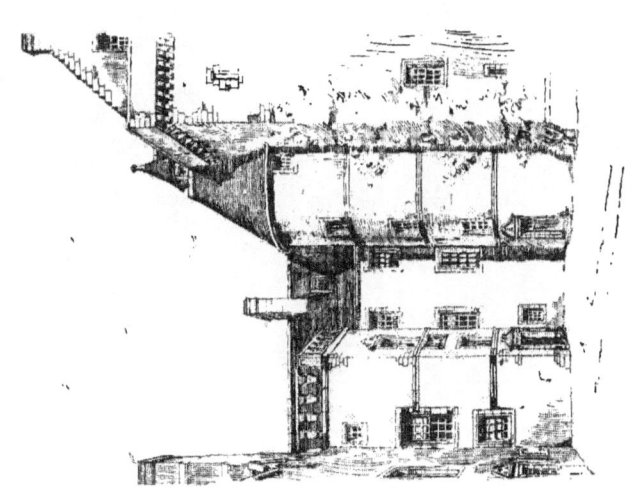

369. *Cessnock Castle, Ayrshire. A corner in the Courtyard*
THOMAS LEADBETTER, Architect.

Royal Scottish Academy Exhibition, 1894.

1596.   *St. Augustine's Church, Sudbury, Suffolk*, LEONARD STOKES, Architect.

THE ROYAL SCOTTISH ACADEMY EXHIBITION, 1894.

517. *Design for Proposed Decoration of Old Hall*, THOMAS BONNAR, Architect.

513.   *Victory*, ROBERT HOPE.

289.   *Decorative Panel, on the new Premises of the Sun Insurance Office, Glasgow*, BIRNIE RHIND, A.R.S.A., Sculptor.

87. *Monument to be erected in Paisley to the Memory of the late Mr. Thomas Coates,*
BIRNIE RHIND, A.R.S.A., Sculptor.

526.　*New Macfadyen Memorial Church, near Manchester,* FRANK W. SIMON AND TWEEDIE, Architects.

390. *Street Architecture, Merchiston—In course of erection for the Chisholm Trust,* DUNN AND FINDLAY, Architects.

524. *Pinkieburn, Midlothian,* G. WASHINGTON BROWNE, A.R.S.A., Architect.

523. *Lochranza Hotel, Arran, for His Grace the Duke of Hamilton, K.T.,* JOHN JAMES BURNET, A.R.S.A.
(MESSRS. JOHN BURNET, SON AND CAMPBELL), Architect.

F

527. *Established Church, Largs (Competitive Design),* JOHN JAMES BURNET, A.R.S.A.
(MESSRS. JOHN BURNET, SON AND CAMPBELL), Architect.

518. *Victoria Tower, Municipal Buildings, Greenock,* H. AND D. BARCLAY, Architects.

525. *Design for Established Church, Juniper Green*, J. ANDERSON WILLIAMSON, A.R.I.B.A., Architect.

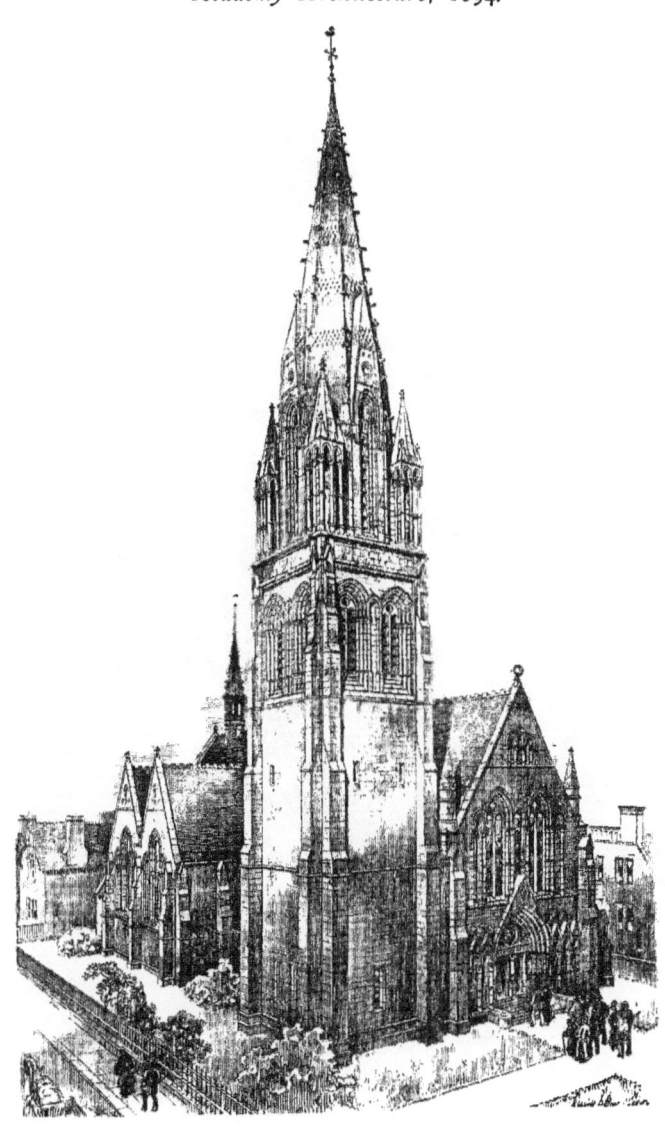

367. *Mayfield Free Church, as now in course of completion,* HIPPOLYTE J. BLANC, A.R.S.A., Architect.

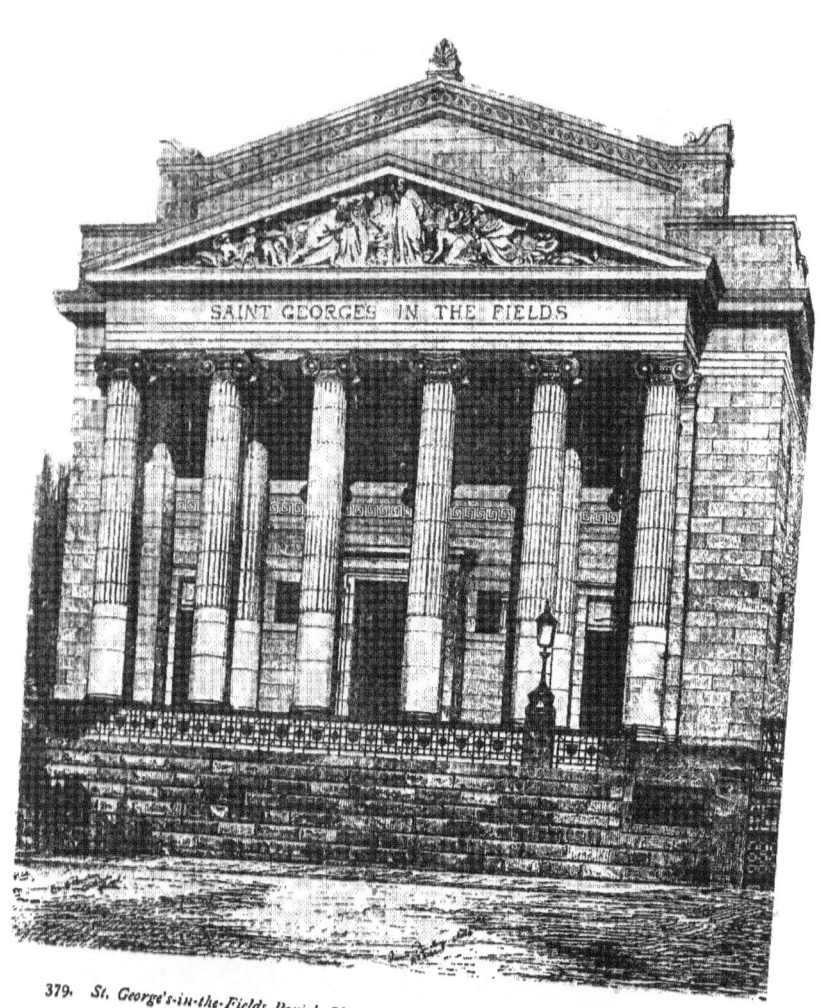

379. *St. George's-in-the-Fields Parish Church, Glasgow,* H. AND D. BARCLAY, Architects.

THE GLASGOW INSTITUTE OF THE FINE ARTS EXHIBITION. 1894.

867. *Canal Boatmen's Institute, Port Dundas,* JOHN HONEYMAN AND KEPPIE, Architects.

846. *St. Andrew's Free Church, Ayr, Competition Design,* W. G. ROWAN, Architect.

859. *Proposed Parish Church, Nairn,* THOMSON AND SANDILANDS, Architects.

875. *Interior of Hall, Moredun, Paisley,* WILLIAM LEIPER, A.R.S.A., Architect.

875. *Interior Drawing Room, Clarendon, Helensburgh,* WILLIAM LEIPER, A.R.S.A., Architect.

876. *Titwood Established Church*, H. E. CLIFFORD, Architect.

858. *Bridgegate, Glasgow*, drawn by WILSON BEATON, Architect.

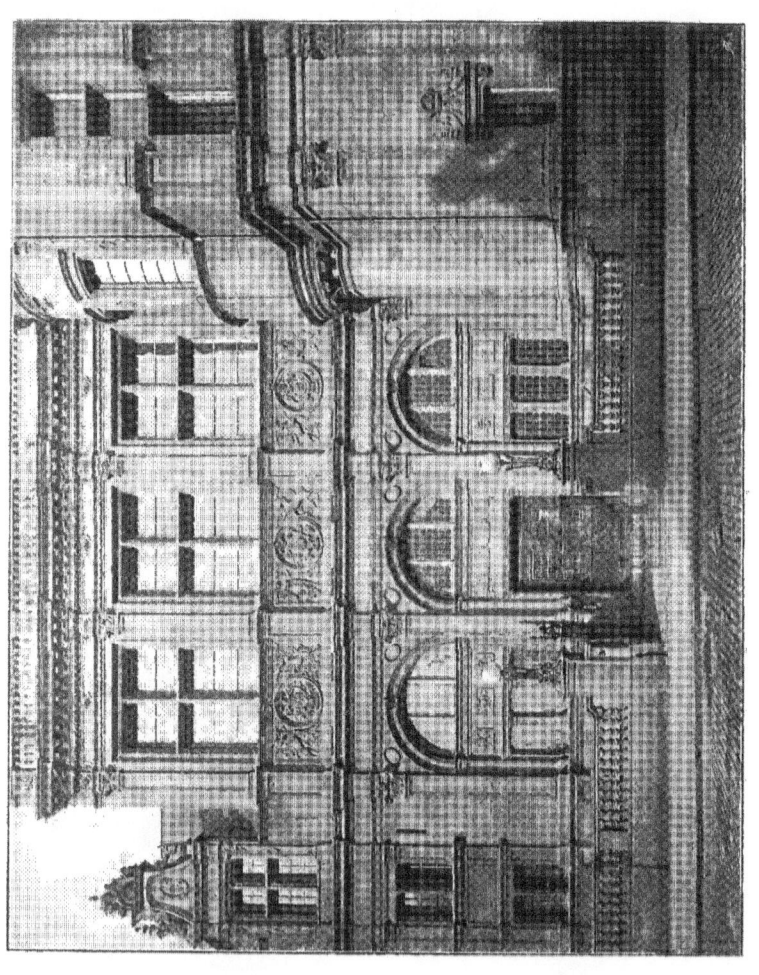

888.   *Edinburgh Public Library*, J. WASHINGTON BROWNE, A.R.S.A., Architect.

847. *Dubhgharadh Lodge, Arran, as proposed to be altered for His Grace the Duke of Hamilton, K.T.*, JOHN JAMES
BURNET, A.R.S.A. (MESSRS. JOHN BURNET, SON, AND CAMPBELL), Architect.

836. *Hutchesontown Free Church, Glasgow,* JOHN B. WILSON, A.R.I.B.A., Architect.

868. *Glasgow Herald Buildings, Mitchell Street*, JOHN HONEYMAN AND KEPPIE, Architects.

869. *Business Premises for Messrs. Redfern, Ltd.,* G. WASHINGTON BROWNE, A.R.S.A., Architect.

856. *Arngask Library, Glenfarg, Perthshire,* ALEX. N. PATERSON, M.A., Architect.

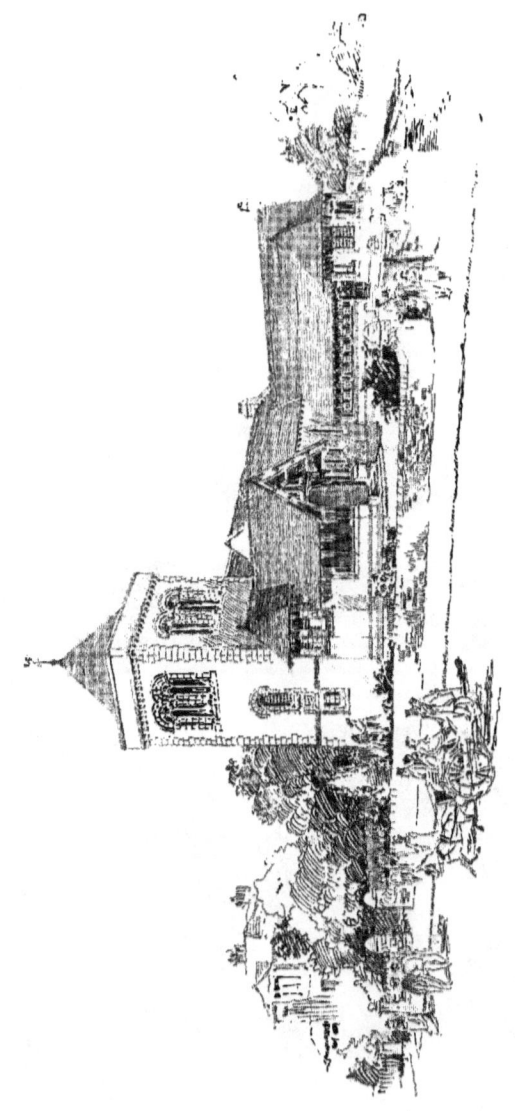

847.   *Dundas U. P. Church, Grangemouth*, JOHN BURNET, SON, AND CAMPBELL, Architects.

855. *The East Lodge, Dunalastair,* THOMAS LEADBETTER, Architect.

873.   *View of Billiard Room, Gallowhill, Renfrewshire,* W. FORREST SALMON, F.R.I.B.A., Architect.

873.   *View of Billiard Room, Gallowhill, Renfrewshire,* W. FORREST SALMON, F.R.I.B.A., Architect.

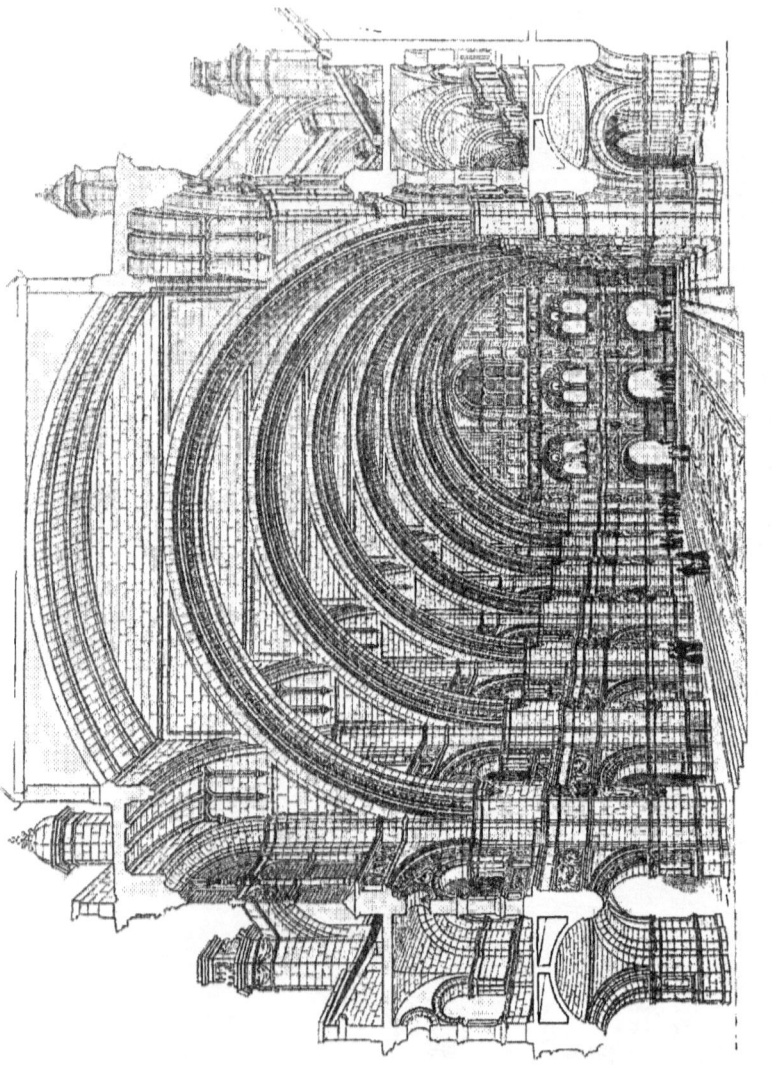

842. *Perspective View of the Interior, Central Hall, Glasgow Art Gallery (Competition),* THOMAS MANLY DEANE (SIR THOMAS NEWENHAM DEANE AND SON), Architect.

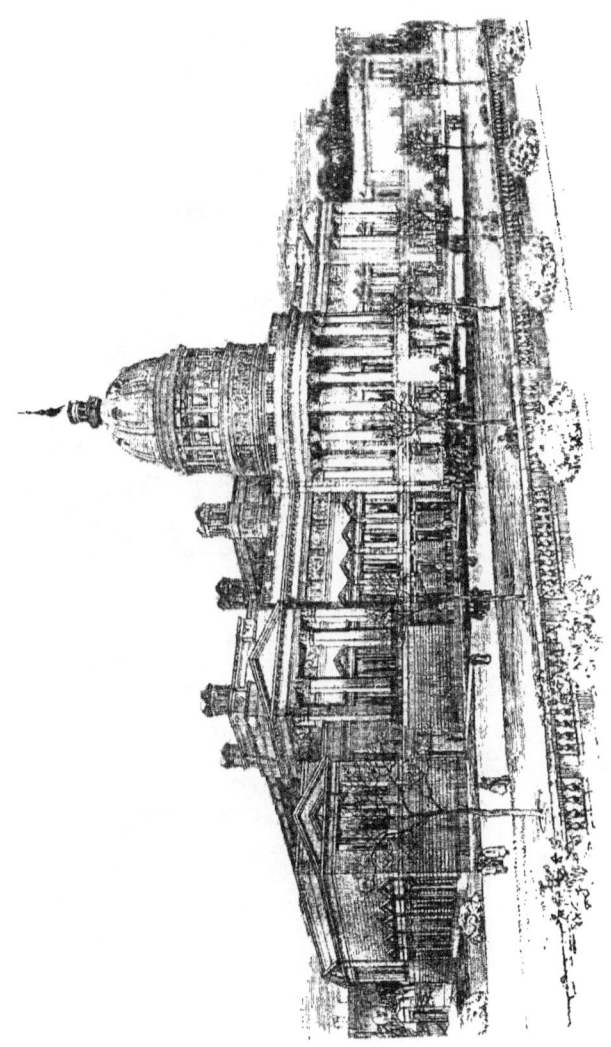

870. *Perspective of Design submitted for Glasgow Art Galleries*, H. AND D. BARCLAY, Architects.

853 *Juniper Green Church (Competition Design),* W. G. ROWAN, Architect.

866. *Juniper Green Church*, JOHN B. WILSON, A.R.I.B.A., Architect.

827. *New Offices of the Scottish Temperance League, Hope Street, Glasgow,*
W. FORREST SALMON, F.R.I.B.A., Architect.

847.   *Established Church, Corrie, in the Island of Arran*, JOHN BURNET, SON, AND CAMPBELL, Architects.

847. *Works Proposed and Executed in the Island of Arran*, JOHN BURNET, SON, AND CAMPBELL, Architects.

Memorial Reredos, Purbrook Church, Hants, J. COATES CARTER, Architect.

818. *Almar, Bute,* STEEL AND BALFOUR, Architects.

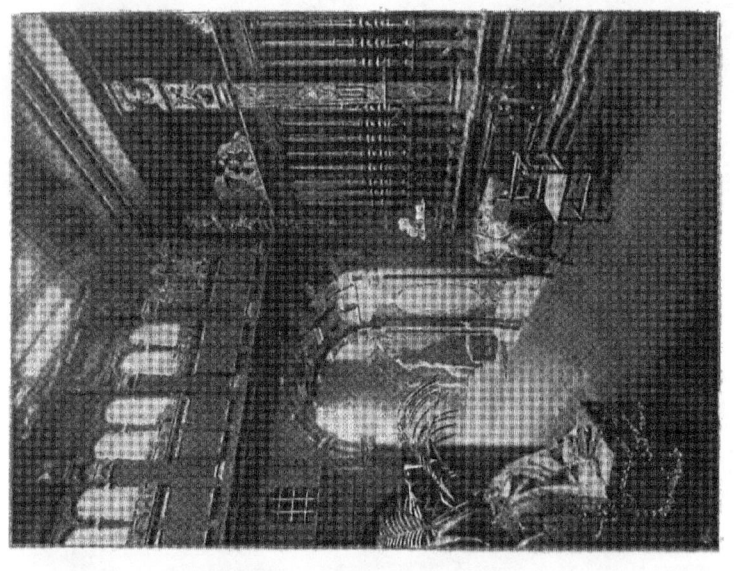

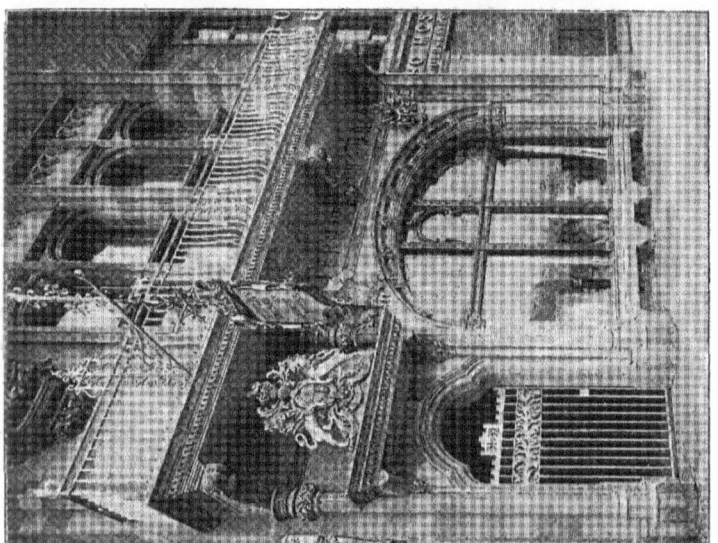

869. *Business Premises for Messrs. Reffern, Ltd., Interior and Exterior,* G. WASHINGTON BROWNE, A.R.S.A.
Architect.

Hydraulic Passenger Lift.—The Otis Elevator Company, Ltd , 4, Queen Victoria Street, E.C.

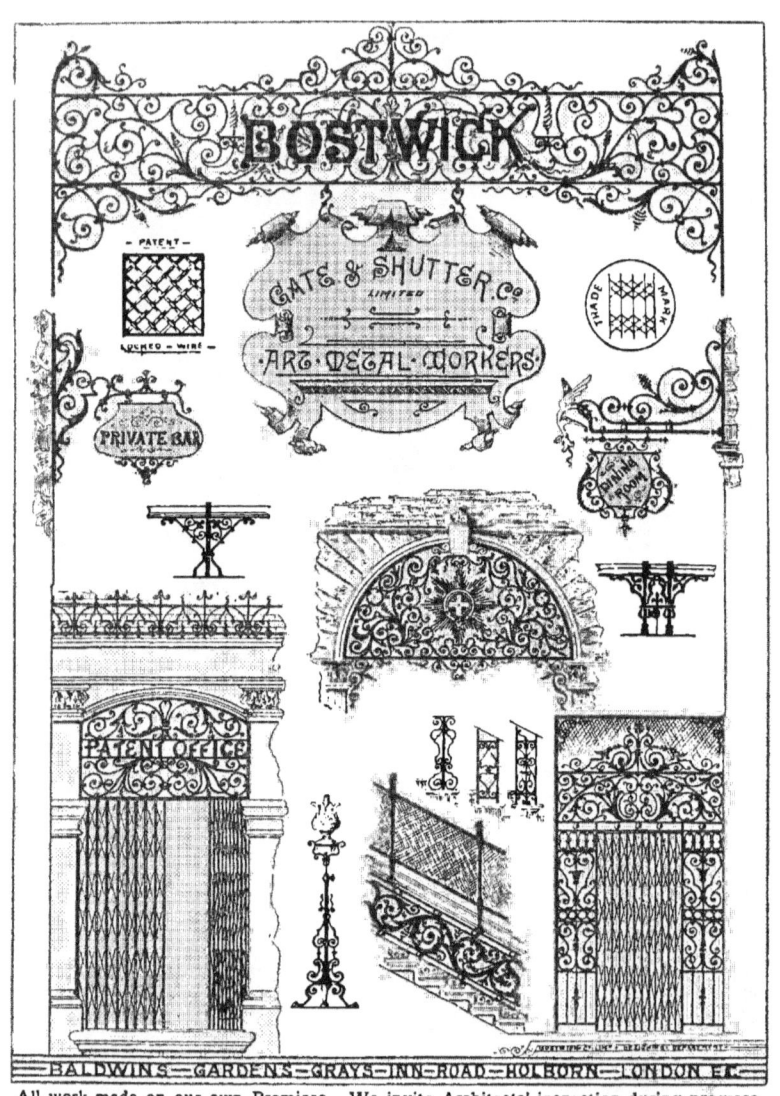

All work made on our own Premises. We invite Architects' inspection during progress.
Architects' Designs carefully worked out. Estimates and Designs for all classes of work in any Metal.

THE BOSTWICK GATE AND SHUTTER CO., Limited,
BALDWIN'S GARDENS, GRAY'S INN ROAD LONDON, E.C.

ANNUAL ARCHITECTURAL REVIEW,
1894.

Sketch, PAUL PFANN, Architect, Tech. Hochschule, Munich.

Hotel, Sandgate, W. H. SETH-SMITH, F.R.I.B.A., Architect.

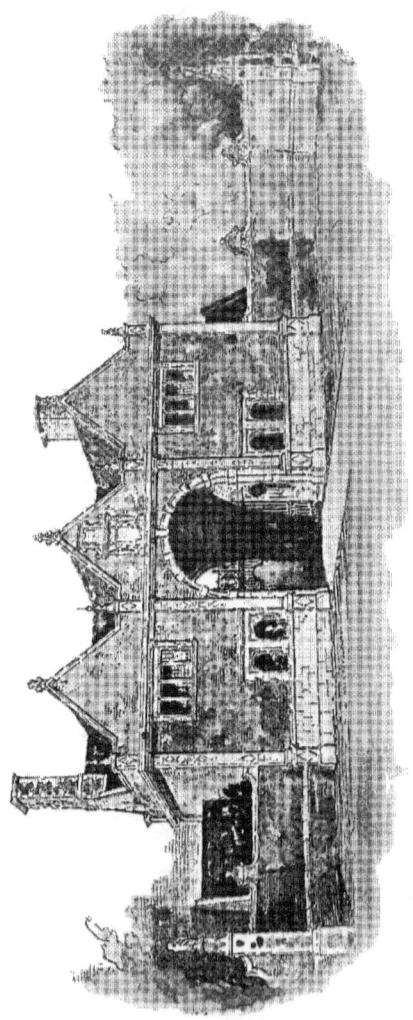

Gate-house, North Mymms, for Walter R. Burns, Esq., ERNEST GEORGE AND PETO, Architects.

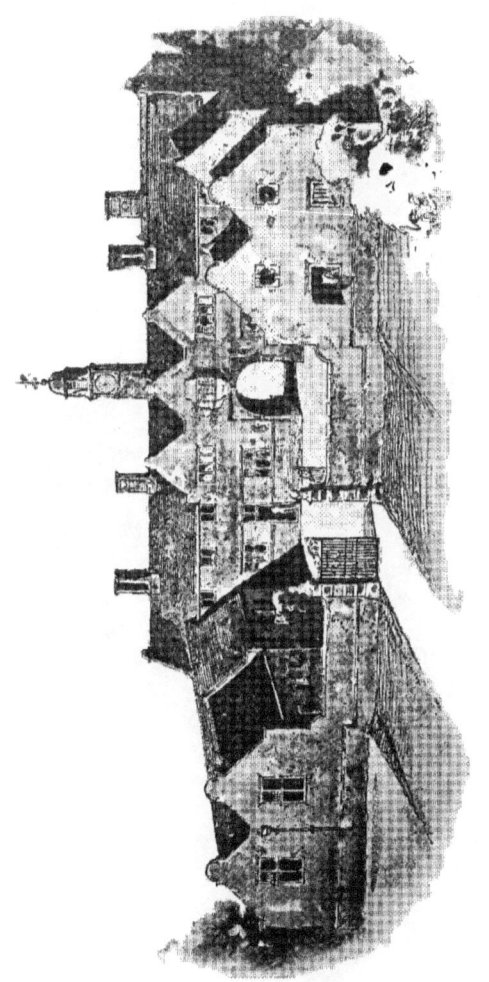

*Stables, **North Mymms,** for Walter R. Burns, Esq.,* ERNEST GEORGE AND PETO, Architects.

Entrance Gateway, Midstone Hall, Hamilton, N.B., ALEXANDER CULLEN, F.S.A. Scot., Architect.

"*The Ross," Hamilton, N.B.*, ALEXANDER CULLEN, F.S.A. Scot., Architect.

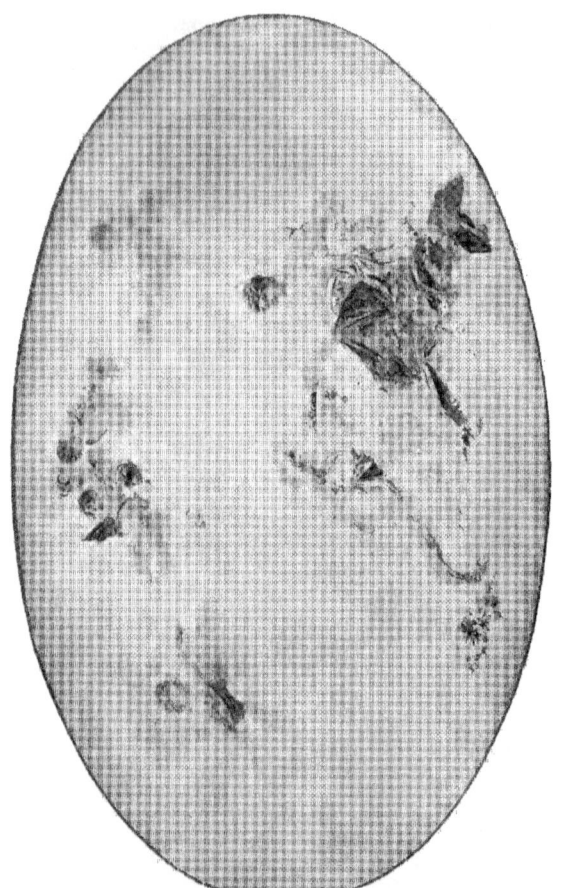

Ceiling Decoration, Hotel Regent, designed and drawn by FREDERICK MARSCHALL.

Ceiling Decoration, House in Dayton, Ohio, designed and drawn by TH. L. WILBERG.

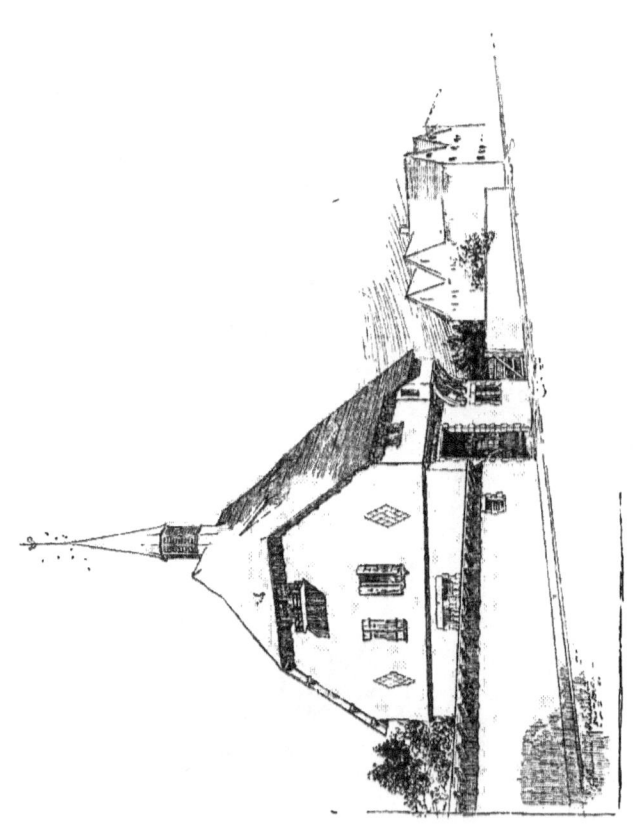

Stable for Dr. Kunyan, South Haven, Mich., CLARENCE A. FULLERTON, Architect.

The Vanderbilt Dormitory, Yale College, CHARLES C. HAIGHT, Architect.

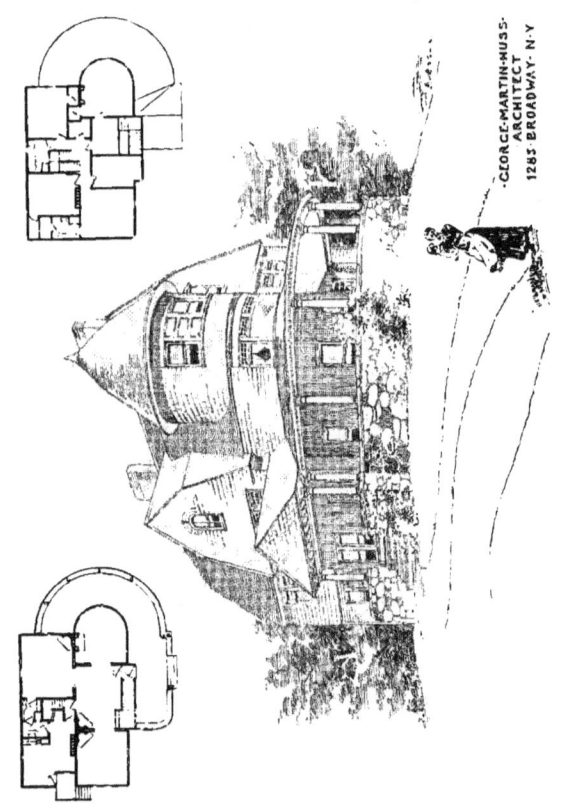

House erected at Rochelle Park, New Rochelle, N.Y., GEO. MARTIN HUSS, Architect.

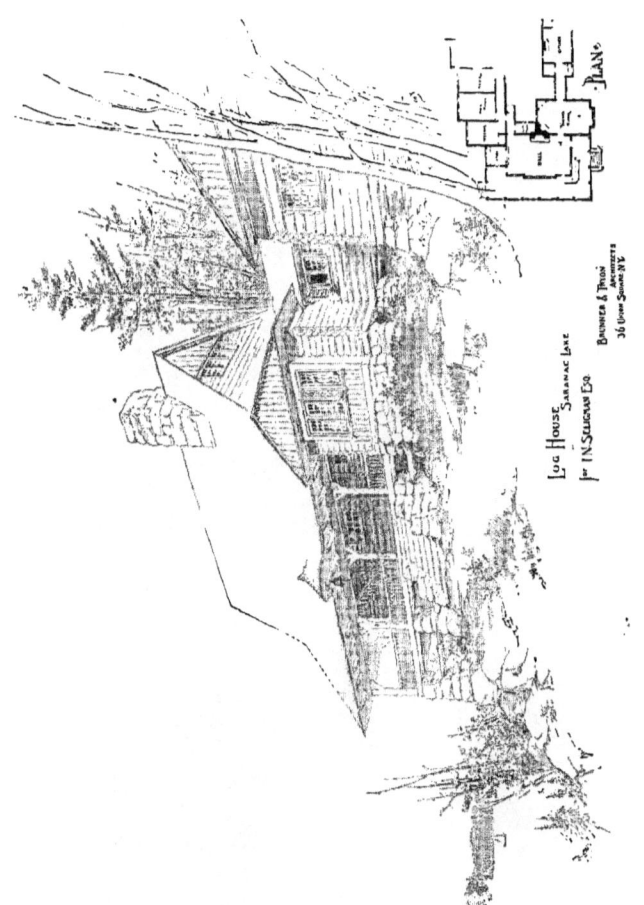

Log House, Saranac Lake, for I. N. Seligman, Esq., BRUNNER AND TRYON, Architects.

Designs for Sigma Phi Chapter House, Williams College, Williamstown, Mass., LAMB AND RICH, Architects.

American Theatre, Forty First Street, New York City, CHARLES C. HAIGHT, Architect.

Hall in House for Mrs. Simeon M. Andrews, Greenwich, Conn., LITTLE AND O'CONNOR, Architects.

New Board School, Zürich, Switzerland, to accommodate 1,200 Girls aged 6-16 years, North-West View, ALEX. KOCII, Architect, London.

(For Plans, *see* pp. 153, 154.)

New Board School, Zürich, Switzerland, to accommodate 1,200 *Girls aged* 6-16 *years, Side Entrance,* ALEX. KOCH,
Architect, London.

(For Plans, *see* pp. 153, 154.)

Life Insurance Company's Offices, Utrecht, J. VERHEUL DZN, Architect, Rotterdam.

Business Premises and Dwelling House of L. Bernheimer, Commerzienrath. Maximiliansplatz, Munich,
PROFESSOR FRIEDRICH THIERSCH AND MARTIN DÜLFER, Architects, Munich.

Metropole, Business Premises, Zürich, H. ERNST, Architect, Zürich.

Corner König Johannstrasse-Galleriestrasse, Dresden, SCHILLING AND GRAEBNER, Architects, Dresden.
(For Plan, *see* p. 153.)

Dwelling House for Herrn Avenarius and Dr. Paul Schumann, SCHILLING AND GRAEBNER, Architects, Dresden.

(For Plan, *see* p. 153.)

Villa Kleyer, Frankfurt, II. TH. SCHMIDT, Architect, Frankfurt a/M·

Villa Garny, Frankfurt, H. TH. SCHMIDT, Architect, Frankfurt a/M.

Pulpit in Church at Radebeul, SCHILLING AND GRAEBNER, Architects, Dresden.

New Synagogue, Milan, Interior, LUCA BELTRAMI, Architect, Milan.
(For Exterior, *see* p. 73, 1890 vol.)

Mausoleum der Familie Fröss zu Zborowitz, Mähren,
MAX FLEISCHER, Architect, Vienna.

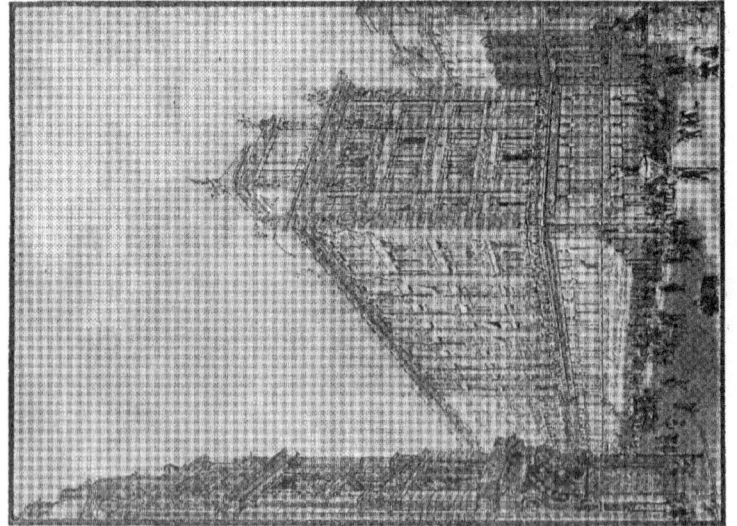

" Der Anker" Life and Annuity Insurance Company's New Offices in Vienna,
OTTO WAGNER, Hon. Corr. Member, R.I.B.A., Architect, Vienna.

(For Plan, *see* p. 144.)

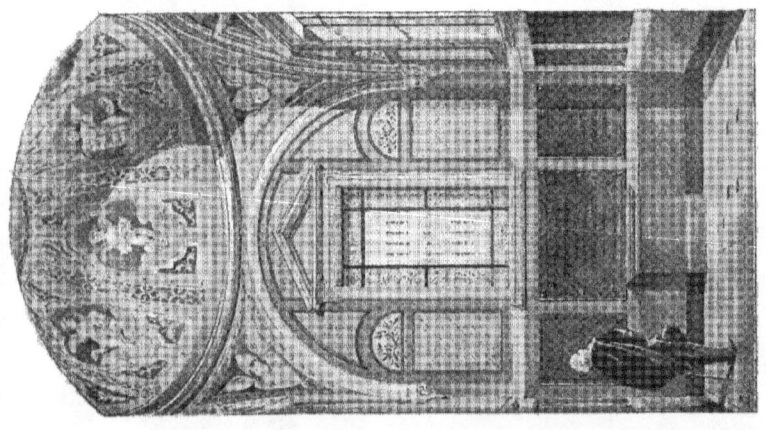

Interior of Synagogue in Vienna, IX., MAX FLEISCHER, Architect, Vienna.

Mausoleum der Familie Fritss zu Zborcnitz, Mähren, Interior,

Court Museum, Vienna, Vestibule on First Floor, THE LATE PROFESSOR CARL FREIHERR VON HASENAUER
Architect.

Court Museum, Vienna. Dome as seen from Vestibule on First Floor, THE LATE PROFESSOR
CARL FREIHERR VON HASENAUER, Architect.

Court Museum, Vienna, Entrance Vestibule, The Late Professor CARL FREIHERR VON HASENAUER, Architect.

Court Museum, Vienna, Principal Staircase, The Late Professor CARL FREIHERR VON HASENAUER, Architect.

Court Museum, Vienna, Principal Staircase, THE LATE PROFESSOR CARL FREIHERR VON HASENAUER, Architect.

Châlet Bodch, Zürich Flüntern, JACQ. GROSS, Architect, Zürich.

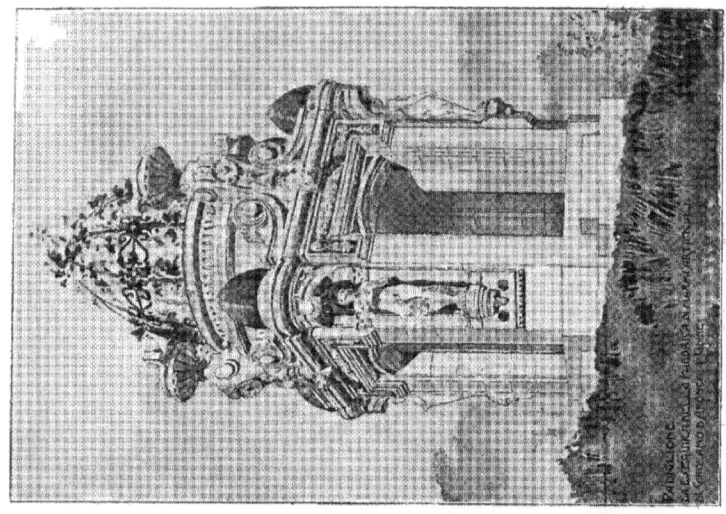

Pavilion at Udine,

Tobacco Kiosque at the Art Exhibition, Venice,

R. D'ARONCO, Architect, Constantinople.

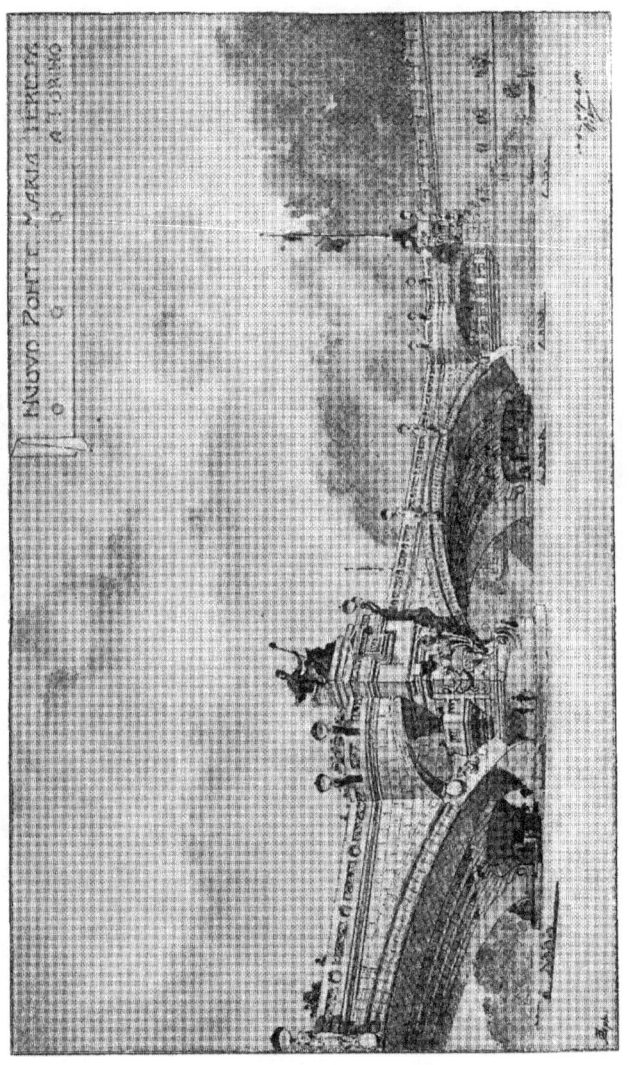

Nuovo Ponte Maria Teresa a Torino, R. D'ARONCO, Architect, Constantinople.

House at Düsseldorf for Herrn Franz Haniel, KAYSER AND VON GROSZHEIM, Architects, Berlin.

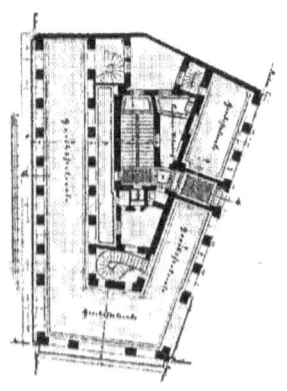

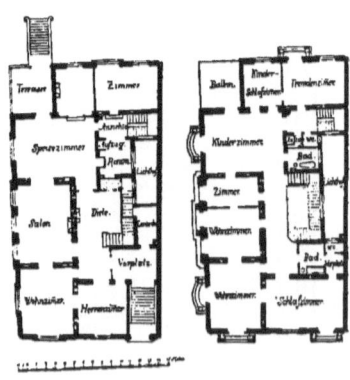

For Elevation, *see* p. 134.

Villa Haniel, plans.

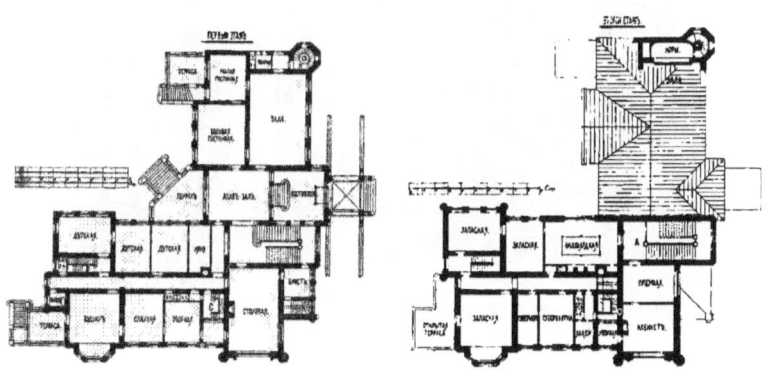

Palais Morozoff, Moskau, F. SCHAECHTEL, Architect, Moskau.

Family House, St. Petersburg, PROFESSOR VICTOR SCHRÖTER, Architect, St. Petersburg.

Church in Gatschino, J. STEPHANITZ, Architect.

Chapel, M. HÄUSLER, Architect.

Memorial Chapel, G. BARANOFFSKY, Architect.

Volks Kuche, St. Petersburg, A. KRUSSOFFSKY, Architect,

Iron Memorial Church, PETROWO-ROPETT, Architect.

New Cemetery for the City of Chiavari, PROFESSOR GAETANO MORETTI, Architect, Milan.

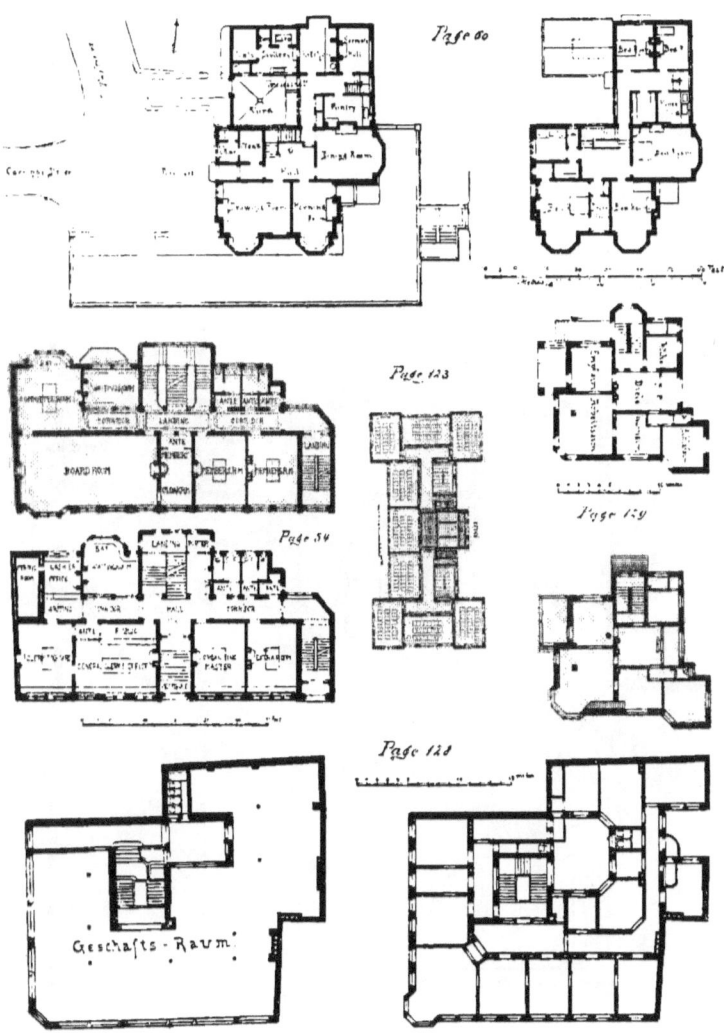

PLANS.—*For Elevations see pages given above.*

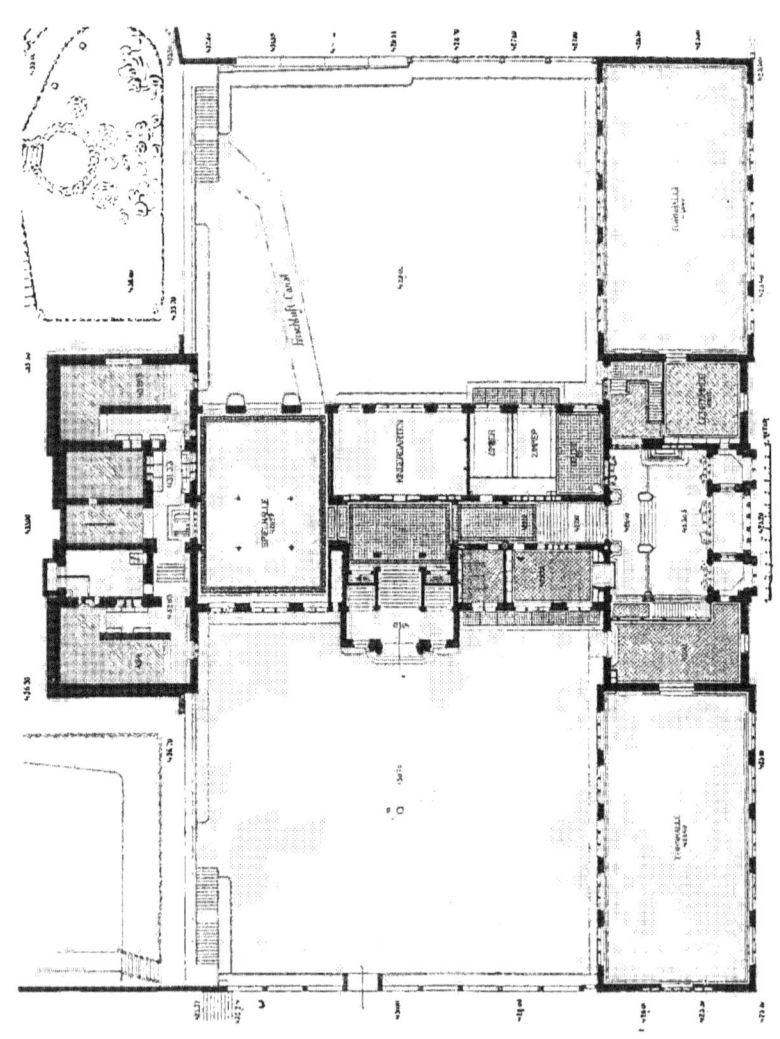

Plans, New Board School, Zürich, Switzerland, ALEX. KOCH, Architect, London.

www.ingramcontent.com/pod-product-compliance
Lightning Source LLC
Chambersburg PA
CBHW021126020726
47500CB00003B/950